ONCE UPON A

BAD HOMBRE

by

Gabriel Hugo

Mission, Texas

Table of Contents

Chapter 1
"DALLAS"

"Whata' we got, Lieutenant?" said Laquita Johnson, the Chief of Police, as she looked up at Lieutenant Ridge entering her office.

"Just this video from the hair salon, Chief. Guy shooting out a TV set."

"So, what are we dealing with? Terrorism? Organized crime? Some disgruntled ex-employee out for revenge? Jealous boyfriend? What?"

Lieutenant Ridge shrugged his shoulders and puckered his lips as he had no good answers to her questions. "Sorry Chief. Don't know yet. Witnesses weren't that much help either. Just as it shows in this video, witnesses said the guy had been sitting around, apparently waiting his turn to get a haircut. Nothing remarkable about him. Suddenly he just got up, pulled a gun and shot the TV shattering it to pieces. Then he turned and walked out without saying a word. No one really got much more detail about him because they were all, as one witness put it, 'shit scared' hiding under chairs and in the restroom. Some simply ran out the door as soon as they saw the gun. Didn't bother to look at the guy."

"Let me get this straight," said the Chief as she stood and slowly walked around her desk only to lean on its front side. She looked at the floor as she continued speaking with Lieutenant Ridge, "Guy gets up, pulls a gun and shoots off a few rounds in the middle of a room full of people and folks don't see anything but the TV being blown to pieces?"

"No kidding, Chief. I was as surprised as you. A lady who was there even went as far as cursing the guy not for shooting the gun in a public area, but because he shot the TV just as she was watching her favorite Mexican soap opera while waiting for her perm to take hold."

The Chief paused briefly, looked up at Lieutenant Ridge immersed in thought and said, "A Mexican soap opera? That's what was playing on the TV?"

"Apparently…at least according to that lady."

"Hmmm…"

"What is it, Chief? You think that had anything to do with the shooting?"

The Chief seemed to simply ignore the question, lost in her thoughts. But after some moments she responded, "…It's a possibility. Or maybe the guy went in there looking for a certain someone who works there. He must have gotten pissed at not seeing them come in that day and shot the TV out of frustration, or to send a message…Or maybe he's just a crazy nut with mental disorders that thought the characters on the television were talking to him, telling him to do crazy things, so he shot the TV to silence the voices. Some schizo like that.

There's just no telling. Go back and interview everyone who was there. Someone has to know something about this guy. Get a good picture of him from the film and run it through all databases."

The Lieutenant looked at his Chief wondering if the situation might call for a full-blown investigation. "Chief," said Lieutenant Ridge questioningly, "all that for a little mayhem? No one was hurt."

Chief Johnson turned around and slowly walked back to take the seat at her desk, all the while addressing the Lieutenant's suggestion in a leisurely and deliberate manner: "I heard of another similar case out in the Phoenix area. Except this guy didn't just go shoot a TV. He went into a packed movie theatre and shot people at random, killing some, wounding others."

She paused. The Lieutenant hesitated then asked, "You think we're dealing with the same guy here, Chief?"

"No," responded the Chief dryly. "That one turned out to be some Alt-right Nazi jerkoff. He was taken into custody shortly after the shooting..."

The Chief sat behind her desk and leaned forward over the desktop looking at the Lieutenant straight in the eyes so as to mince no words, "This guy on the tape looks like a Mexican. Maybe some cartel hitman, or maybe just some asshole out for some mayhem. Either way, I'll be damned if I'm gonna let some *bad hombre* come and terrorize my city!" Chief

Johnson's cold but familiar stare made her directives unmistakably clear, yet she continued,

"I'm sure you are aware of the reason why I called you to my office, Lieutenant. Captain Moore has lobbied quiet strongly on your behalf and I tend to trust his judgement. I just need to know from your own mouth if you plan to honor his support or if you'll betray his confidence in you regarding that *other* situation?"

For a second, Lieutenant Ridge looked like a fish out of water, struggling to breathe. He pursed his lips, exhaled through the nose, and as his eyes wandered on their way down toward the floor he replied,

"Yes, ma'am...I mean, no, ma'am. I do not plan to let the Captain down. Or the department, for that matter. That other situation is a thing of the past."

The Chief zeroed in on Lieutenant Ridge's face inspecting it for any sign of deliberate misleading, but after a moment she eased up and dismissed the Lieutenant with,

"Good. Keep me posted."

"Yes, ma'am," said the Lieutenant dutifully as he retreated backwards out of the office.

Lieutenant Ridge went straight past all his fellow officers and department staff until he exited the building. When he reached his car out in the parking lot he got in and sat there for a while thinking. In his head a string of images of a little girl swirled around, plaguing him as they had been for ten months now. She was stiff, pale, naked, and had been tossed away onto a pile of leaves and grass in a wooded area along Ronald Reagan Memorial Highway. The paleness of her skin was one of the things that caught Lieutenant Ridge's eye. It seemed to be covered in grey powder. He had run a finger over one of her arms and taken a sample of the grey matter. It looked like ashes. What reason had there been for her to be covered in ash? He had no idea, forgetting in the moment the fact that he had seen ash fall in town just a few days before. Nonetheless, he thought that maybe the ash was something that could point to a quirk of the killer.

Postmortem analysis showed the victim had been raped repeatedly, as if there'd been several men involved. Cause of death was due to strangulation. She was only six years old at the time of her murder. Lieutenant Ridge struggled daily to erase the images of that small, fragile body so ruthlessly mangled and abused. As a father of a little girl of the same age, he could not bear to think what his life would become if his daughter ever had to suffer a fate like that anonymous victim. So far, there had been no evidence found pointing to a suspect, and no one had come forward to claim the body. Given the apparent ethnic background of the girl, it was possible she was an undocumented immigrant. After all, that highway was a known corridor for trafficking of drugs and people.

The case had gone cold, but for Lieutenant Ridge the sight of the girl's eyes as they flipped her little corpse over to look at her face, would haunt him for the rest of his life. They were inanimate, glassy, hollow, and cold eyes that begged him to not give up on her case.

This was the guiding principle behind the Lieutenant's constant questioning of the Department's allocation of resources to seemingly unimportant or insignificant cases such as this most recent one of the TV shooter. But the Chief had been quite clear as to her wishes, and besides, she had already come down hard on his boss, Captain Ray Moore, on two previous occasions about "wasting" Department resources by allowing his officers to pursue a dead-end case.

Lieutenant Ridge came back out of his all-consuming thoughts, started the engine, and headed straight to the hair salon to follow up with the owner in case she had remembered other details of the television shooting incident. This would make the Chief happy, he thought. Or at least it would get her off his back thinking that he now was completely off the dead girl's case and fully committed to following her orders.

At the salon, Lieutenant Ridge noticed that the business was shut down. On the glass door at the entrance a sign hung simply stating that the place was "CLOSED (until further notice)," and "Sorry for the Inconvenience". On his mobile phone the Lieutenant retrieved the number he had gotten from the owner of the salon and tried calling it not knowing that it was the line to the very same location where he stood. The owner did not give him her own mobile phone number. After several attempted calls which only led to an answering service, he gave up. Lieutenant Ridge was about to head back to his car, but then noticed that the small insurance company office next to the salon was open for business, so he decided to pay them a visit on the off chance that someone there might be friends with the salon owner and could possibly have her personal number.

"Sorry, I don't have her number. I don't even know her. We've crossed paths a few times and say hi to each other, but that's it," said the insurance agent from behind her unusually large, heavily varnished, wooden desk. It seemed out of place for the type of business it was in. Somehow, it seemed to the Lieutenant that the desk would be more fitting in a D.A.'s office or even in his own boss's office. Not that he thought they truly deserved it, but perhaps a bit more than the unassuming insurance salesperson in front of him.

"Okay," he responded. "The day of the incident in her salon there was no one at this business. Aren't you open every weekday?"

"Yes. But that day I had a training to attend, and since I am currently understaffed, I had to close down for the day."

"Well, then. Thank you for your help," said Lieutenant Ridge. As he turned to head out of the office, he paused and looked back at the insurance agent one more time extending his arm. "Here's a couple of my business cards. If you see her soon, please tell her to contact me. I had given her one but people misplace things easily. Especially after being involved in traumatic events."

The insurance agent looked at the Lieutenant with a smile accepting his cards but then her facial expression turned to one of sudden realization as her eyes popped out and her mouth dropped.

"Oh, my god. I'm so stupid! Sorry, officer. Here you go," she said pulling an envelope from her desk drawer and placing it in the Lieutenant's hand. "Yesterday a man came in asking about the salon's owner, too. He seemed to me like he was just curious or a concerned citizen. He told me he had heard about what happened and wanted to reach out to the owner. He asked if I could give her this envelope. I was going to say no, but he was a big guy, kind of intimidating. So, I said okay. Didn't ask questions. I thought, since the envelope is open, it must be harmless. But I really don't want to have that kind of responsibility. I prefer if you hold onto it until you see her."

Lieutenant Ridge, highly intrigued, approached the large wooden desk again taking the envelope from the insurance agent's hand.

"This man," he said. "What did he look like?"

"Well, big guy. Hispanic. Had a big, bushy beard. Almost looked fake, if you ask me. Long, graying hair. Looked like a biker dude..." She threw an arm across her chest and rested her other elbow on it while she rubbed her chin making it obvious she was trying to remember more details.

"Yeah, definitely a biker," she continued. "He had on a black leather jacket, faded jeans and a pair of black cowboy boots. Oh—he also had a pair of Ray-Ban aviator sunglasses."

"Is that all you remember?" asked Lieutenant Ridge.

"Pretty much. Why? Is that not useful to you?"

"Oh, no it's not that. It's just that people seemed to be quite forgetful about what the guy that shot up the place next door looked like. And here you are describing a man to a T. It's a curious thing."

"Well, in this business you have to have quite an eye for details, officer."

"Lieutenant."

"Lieutenant. Sorry."

"It's alright. I guess you might also be able to remember him better since he didn't brandish a huge gun in your face."

The Lieutenant said this as he finished writing some notes on his notepad. He flipped the flaps back in place and slid the pad into his coat pocket as he turned his eyes at the insurance agent. She had run out of things to say and only looked at him expectantly. Lieutenant Ridge simply winked at her and waved a half salute and half goodbye as he was about to make his way out the door. He stopped, stared out through the glass at the flurry of flakes in the wind and said almost to himself,

"It looks like we're getting ashfall again."

****

Chapter 2
"IN THE MAGIC VALLEY"

The mobile news crew prepared themselves for their broadcast to go on the air. As they were standing by on site in the downtown area of McAllen, Texas, a Greyhound bus coming in by way of San Antonio was pulling into the bus station just next door making it somewhat difficult for them to hear the announcer's prerecorded presentation as it came on through everyone's ear pieces while they counted down in their heads:

"From the Valley's KSVT - TV newsroom in Mission, Texas

-The News Leader-

this is

Action 8 News at 10

With Tom de la Cruz

Sports with Jonathan Landon

The Weather with Christian Varon"

Tom de la Cruz, the lead anchorman sitting in the newsroom, saw the producer's hand fall from the side of the camera. His fingers pointing at Tom in the shape of a gun meant the countdown was over and he was live.

"Hello everyone. I'm Tom de la Cruz. This is Action Eight News at ten. Tonight, we have new developments on the case of the *Telenovela Shooter*. As some of you may recall, Action Eight News was first to break the story a full month ago when it had been reported to the authorities that another attack at a public location had occurred in which an individual, who witnesses describe as a Latino middle-aged man, pulled a gun and shot a television set in a crowded public space. Today he has struck again; this time in one of our Valley's own businesses.

Authorities confirmed that this is the third such incident. The first being at a hair salon in Dallas, followed by the second at a Mexican food restaurant in San Antonio. On this latest incident here in the Valley, authorities have concluded that it is likely the same man involved, and that it seems he is headed toward the border. No word yet on a possible motive. However, authorities are quick to point out that no person has been hurt in any of the shootings. We go live now with Mark Lopez who is on the scene of the latest incident. Hello Mark."

Mark Lopez, the correspondent on the street, stood in front of the site nodding his head. He wore a long, black trench coat and a pair of gloves as he looked into the camera holding the microphone on that cold winter night. His cameraman, Carlos, held the camera over his shoulder having removed it from the tripod after taking some stock footage of the area. Mark nodded some more because of the slight delay after Tom introduced him, but then began his report:

"Good evening, Tom. We are here at the Nueva Ola Arts Café in downtown McAllen. We spoke to several of the patrons. All reported the same thing. A Hispanic male, about 6 feet 2 inches walked into the café at about 8 p.m. He seemed to have become irritated when he stepped into a type of conference room at this business, usually reserved for larger parties, where a television set was on and tuned to a Spanish language soap opera, or a *'telenovela'*. The man was seen pulling out a gun and aiming straight at the TV shooting off a round destroying the set. I have here the owner of the café, Mr. Armando Banderas. Mr. Banderas, had you ever seen this man in your establishment prior to this incident?"

"Not at all," Responded the owner of the café, attempting to take the microphone from Mark's hand. "I know most of my clients by name. When new people come in, I take notice right away. This man immediately got my attention as soon as he stepped in the door. You know, it was one of those things when you just know that something ain't right about a person. That's exactly how I felt about him as soon as I laid eyes on him."

Mark firmly pulled his microphone away from Mr. Bandera's hand and asked,

"What was it that set off those red flags in your view?"

"*Pues*, I'm not exactly sure, but it was just something about the way he carried himself, you know? Something about his eyes just wasn't right."

"So, then it is safe to say that you got a good look at him? Could you describe him for us?

"Oh, well *es que*, you know, come to think of it, I don't think I paid much attention to his face. I mean, I looked at his eyes and general appearance. But I wasn't trying to memorize what he looked like. Why would I? It's not like I liked him or anything. I wasn't checking him out. I don't swing that way, *me entiendes*?"

Mr. Banderas appeared to be joking with his homophobic comments as he smirked and winked at Mark who just didn't know how to react to the statement, so he moved on.

"Did he say anything to you or to any of the other patrons that you know of?"

"No," responded Mr. Banderas in a much more restrained and serious tone. "He didn't say anything to me. And apparently no one else talked to him, you know? It was like he just came in for the purpose of shooting up my TV. Really strange...also expensive. I just bought the damned thing. Gotta' file a police report for the insurance *y todo*, man. Real hassle..."

Mark turned back directly facing the camera which shifted away from Mr. Banderas, focusing entirely on the correspondent.

"And there you have it, Tom," said Mark slowly walking away from Mr. Banderas, who appeared eager to share more of his grievances with the news audience.

With Mr. Banderas following closely behind and trying to stay in the shot, Mark continued with his report, saying:

"Again, nothing yet as far as a motive, but some in the McAllen Police Department disclosed to me on condition of anonymity that they believe this may be tied to Mexican drug cartels. Perhaps someone is sending a message to local establishments on this side of the border that there may be a new way of doing business. No longer will business owners enjoy the tranquility of conducting their day-to-day activities without, perhaps, having to pay quote unquote 'rent' to the new heads of these organizations," he said this using air quotes with his fingers, despite having mentioned the punctuation marks aloud.

He concluded his report saying,"... However, most of that is strictly speculation at this point. We will be following this story closely and will keep you and our RGV viewers informed on the latest developments. From downtown McAllen, I am Mark Lopez, Action Eight News. Back to you, Tom..."

As soon as he saw Carlos shut off the light mounted on the camera, Mark knew the transmission was cut. He started rolling up the microphone's long cable which his partner had unplugged from the camera. They were both working fast, in part because that was their last job for the evening and they wanted to go home, and also because they were still being hounded by Mr. Banderas in front of the Nueva Ola Café.

"So what time is my interview going to be aired on the TV?" Asked Mr. Banderas at their backs.

"It was a live broadcast, sir. It already aired," responded Carlos.

Mr. Banderas, appearing quite perplexed, looked at Carlos in awe, then at Mark and back to Carlos again. He could not believe what he heard.

"Are you serious? Oh, man! Why didn't you all tell me? I wanted to record it. It was my first TV interview. And right in front of my business. Are you kidding me? That would be awesome as promotion on my website. You guys really botched it on this one. *La cagaron*, bros'."

At this, Mark swiftly turned around peering wide-eyed at the café owner. He was about to cuss him out but Carlos, knowing his partner to be a bit of a short fuse, stepped right back in saying,

"Not to worry, sir. Here is my card. Just email me at this address and I will be happy to forward you the link to our website when I upload the video. It will be on there for at least a month. I'm sure you can just link it to your website and get your patrons to check it out quick and easy."

"Yeah. I like that. Quick and easy. At-a-boy. *Tu si sabes, carnal. Orale, pues,* thank you very much. I will be emailing you tonight. *Gracias, chavos. Los watcho!*" Mr. Banderas shouted as he skipped away back inside his café with a big smile on his face.

"Can you believe that son-of-a-bitch?" was the first thing out of Mark's mouth as soon as they saw the door closing behind Mr. Banderas.

"I know, huh?" said Carlos.

They boarded their equipment into the van and got in. Carlos in the driver's seat. Mark in the passenger's side. He was scrolling through his Facebook feed on his phone as he heard Carlos speak after a brief silence.

"You think that guy really is someone sent by the cartels, bro?"

"Hmm?" Mark responded completely absentmindedly. He wanted to respond to some notifications, but his partner often got chatty after covering a story. Mark reluctantly put down his phone and finally offered a complete response.

"Don't know. Maybe. It's not like these guys are confined to operating only in Mexico. No matter how many border patrol agents there are or how big a border wall they build, these guys are running multinational drug corporations. They have the means to get to anyone, anywhere, you know what I mean?" said Mark looking straight through the windshield at the streetlamps along 17th Street.

"Yeah, but I don't think it's the cartels, to tell you the truth."

"Oh, really?"

"Yeah," asserted Carlos.

"Well, then, what is it? Do tell."

"It's a reckoning."

"A whaaa?" asked Mark accentuating the question in jest.

"I'm serious. A reckoning, man. That's what this is."

"What are you talking about, 'Carlitos *güey*'?" Now his partner was outright mocking Carlos with that play on words sounding like the title of the movie "Carlito's Way" but meaning something like "dumb Carlitos". It was Mark's classic go-to rag on him whenever he was being slightly facetious.

"A settling of accounts, my friend. That's what that is. Haven't you ever heard of the prophecies of Moctezuma?"

"*Moco*-what?!" said Mark, still raking on him.

"*No mames.* Don't tell me you don't know who Moctezuma is?"

"Of course, I know, bro. Just playing with ya." Mark straightened up in his seat and striking a more serious tone, he continued,

"Yeah, I read the prophecy, too. It has been said that there will be a Chicano Television Killer on the loose in the Rio Grande Valley in the 21st century. The prophecy has come to pass! Repent!"

Mark jumped out of his seat in a fit of laughter having said this. He alternated between slapping the dashboard in front of him and slapping his knees. It looked like he was swapping off ants from his lap. Carlos cracked a smile and even chuckled raising a middle finger at his news partner.

"Jackass!" said Carlos. "It's for real. It says that after a certain time there is going to be a new sun born, a new people."

"Wait, wait. Let's not throw away this revelation. We got to get this on tape, my friend. Solving the case of the TV shooter!" said Mark with a chuckle as he picked up his phone and began recording his friend.

Carlos again stuck out a middle finger at Mark and proceeded with his account.

"According to the prophecy, there will be a man who will come from the east headed toward Mexico. The real Mexico. Tenochtitlan. He is supposed to usher in the new age of humanity on Earth. One of equality and love. Not like it is now with inequality and hate everywhere."

"Bro, I *hate* to break it to you, but the guy is a simple schmo shooting TV sets, bruh. He ain't ushering in nothing but a small prison sentence for himself. Unless he ends up killing someone. Then he's fucked for life. 'Cuz ya don't mess with Texas, boy! Besides, the guy is operating here in the states, bro. We're not in Mexico."

"Sure. But look at his trajectory. He started in Dallas. And where is that? In the east. Northeast of here to be exact, but still technically it's east. Then he hit San Antonio. Now the Valley. He's obviously on a south-bound track...straight down to old Mexico."

Mark put down his phone. Laughter spent. Taking a deep breath, he readjusted himself in his seat facing forward and said,

"Yeah, well. You never know. Everything's possible. But it's probably just one of those bad hombres the right-wing nuts talk about all the time. C'mon, let's get back to the station and drop off the van. I want to get home. I'm freezing my balls off out here."

Carlos turned the key in the ignition, which brought on the headlights illuminating the street ahead. He was about to shift into gear when he paused and looked intently out through the windshield.

"Oh, damn. Looks like we're getting snow tonight."

Mark looked up at him then out ahead toward the light in front of them. Indeed, there were flakes falling.

"I didn't know there was snow in the forecast," said Mark. "It's the fucking Valley. If there was snow coming, we would have known about it. Thrown a fucking *pachanga* over it. Canceled classes and shit."

Carlos simply nodded in agreement and said, "I guess old weatherman Varon really doesn't know what the hell he's talking about when he's doing his weather report after all."

Mark ignored the comment and exited the van. The curiosity in him to inspect the flakes seemed derived from some realization or an intuition. He walked around to the front of the van and put out his hand to catch the falling flakes in the cold night. When he had a fair amount on the palm of his hand, he brought it up to the light and looked at it closely. With his other hand's fingers, he pushed the flakes around crushing them to dust which he took between his fingers. He straightened up to search for Carlos' face and found him looking back at him through the windshield from inside the van. They both looked at each other silently and with puzzled looks for a moment until finally Mark spoke up loudly showing Carlos the smudged flakes on his palm: "Ashes."

****

Bienvenidos A México

Prohibido el transporte de armas de fuego.

Welcome To Mexico

Illegal to transport firearms.

The television set kept losing the signal compelling the eager spectator to continuously have to rise from his seat and attempt to readjust the make-shift antenna crafted out of a wire hanger and placed on the back of the old set.

He had just fixed the signal for the sixth time and was about to sit back down to enjoy his favorite programming when another man's voice interrupted his daily TV ritual. It was one of his assistants and lookouts at that post on the outskirts of the city.

"What is it, *hombre*?!" he demanded, clearly frustrated as he tried to divide his attention between his assistant and his TV set trying not to lose out on the newest episode of his favorite show.

"The boss is coming. He's driving like a mad-man!"

The two men joined together at the door peeking out toward the dirt road where they could barely see their boss's truck barreling down in a thick cloud of dust and debris mixed with the powder of recently fallen ash. It was as if the devil himself were rising out of hell on that cold and dry Mexican afternoon. The two men had only moments to put the place in order, shut off the TV set, and act as if they were busily standing by, high-powered Ar-15s at their sides ready for whenever the boss called them into action.

From inside they could hear the truck's powerful engine roaring louder and louder as it neared their post. Then someone killed the engine and the doors creaked and slammed violently onto the frame of the vehicle. Footsteps could be heard coming down hard on the wooden floor of the front porch as three pairs of boots smashed their way toward the entrance. Before the screen door opened the boss's voice thundered through like a lion's roar cutting across the savannas.

"Capitán!" Shouted the man they called *"Comander."* He was the most feared drug cartel leader along the frontier towns and cities.

"Quien putos es ese avispón pendejo y de a cual panal cayo?" he asked, demanding information from his underling about the man everyone in the news was talking about.

The drug lord was directing his interrogation at his top captain. He was the man who had been struggling with the TV antenna, and who now was standing firmly at attention as the boss finally came into view having entered the house. Often, he referred to this man in some variation of *"El Capitán,"* *"Mi Capitán,"* *"Capi,"* or simply *"Capitán"* depending on the context, the purpose of his call, or his general mood, which was fickle.

*"La verdad...*we don't know, *Comander,"* replied *Capitán.*

The drug lord approached him menacingly, looking him straight in the eyes and probed some more. "What happened, exactly?"

"I spoke to our people at the bus station. They said they saw this guy come out of nowhere shooting up the TV sets. Every single one of them until they were all broken," said *Capitán*.

"And when was this? What time?"

"Yesterday. It was around 7 p.m."

"You say it was around 7? So, it could also have been at 6 or 8? What the hell kind of information is that? You are supposed to be my consigliere," shouted *Comander* at him, shoving him at the shoulder. By this point, he was only an inch away from *Capitán's* face and looking like a fight dog growling under his breath at its opponent instances before the first vicious bite at the neck to start the fight.

"*Perdoneme, patrón*. I meant to say 7 p.m. It was definitely at 7."

"And how can you be so sure now?"

"Well…because…" *Capitán* hesitated as he looked down at the tips of his black leather cowboy boots, as if the answer were hidden under his feet.

"What? What is it?" demanded his boss impatiently. "I don't like suspense. Get to it!

"Well, I am certain because that's the time the *novela "La Pasion de Tu Amor"* comes on. And that's what was playing when I got the call about what was going on."

"You mean to tell me that you are a *novelero*, Capitán? Who would have thought a big, bad motherfucker like you would turn out to be such a softy romantic who watches soaps!"

Comander took a few steps back seeing his captain break under the pressure. He turned back to look at the men in his company and broke into a hearty laughter which spared no breath for a half minute as he flung a series of roundhouse slaps on *Capitán's* backside.

"C'mon, boss. Don't laugh. I have no life outside of my work. That *novela* is my only pastime."

"Ok, ok," responded his boss as he tried to catch his breath. "Personally, I don't give a Xoloitzcuintli's bare ass what it is you do in the privacy of your life. But give me some good news about this situation, *Capitán*. The bus routes have been put on hold while the police investigate. This asshole has put us behind schedule."

"*Pues*, we may be falling behind schedule on delivery but the merchandize is fully intact, *Comander*. None of the mules were hurt or killed. And the buses are also still fully loaded."

"So, then, if he didn't target the mules, or the merchandize, or the buses themselves, then what the fuck was he after?"

"The truth is we just don't know, boss. One of the men said he had heard of this guy before, but that he was mainly operating in the U.S. What he is doing here I do not know."

"I bet you he was sent out there by that bastard *El Zapo Tote*. That asshole and his entire organization have had a hard-on for my business enterprise since I sent *El Viejo* to the hole. But if they think I'm just going to bend over and touch my ankles while they butt-fuck this whole operation, they got another thing coming."

"But I don't get it, *Comander*. Why would this guy show up and just shoot at TVs and get lost in the crowd?"

"You don't get it?" the boss stopped mid step as he had been pacing back and forth trying to decipher the meaning of the incident at his bus depot. He looked at *Capitán* and said,

"It's a message. Clear as day. We either tune in or tune out. See what I'm saying? They want the power to control the whole show. But I am the lead actor, director, and producer of this *pinche* show. So, fuck those sons of bitches. They want war? They got war!"

The drug lord walked back up to *Capitán* and positioned himself squarely in front of him.

"Mi Capitán!" he ordered his underling to attention.

Capitán immediately dropped the butt of his weapon onto the floor standing it up next to him and holding it by the tip of the barrel besides his left leg. He flung his right hand up to his forehead as a soldier would do when saluting his commander in chief shouting, "Yes, sir!"

"I want you to assemble a team of specialists. We are going to settle our little dispute once and for all. I want you to hit them by tomorrow night!"

"Sir, yes sir! Permission to ask a question, boss."

"What is it?"

"It's about the stranger, sir. What about the shooter at the bus station?"

"That asshole is of no consequence. I don't play for pawns. Kings are the ones I topple. Make sure you take every precaution and make all the necessary arrangements. You fail this and you can say your final goodbyes to your family. Do you understand?

"Sir, absolutely, sir! I swear on my mother's life I will not fail, boss."

"By the way," said *Comander* as he was about to make his way back to the truck. "…find out just who the hell keeps burning so much trash. The whole rode is covered up in ashes! Find them and put them out of commission, you hear me?"

"Yes sir."

Hours later, *Capitán* and his squad arrived at a large warehouse located in the center of town in what the organization called the "*Zona Verde*" or "Green Zone" copying the international zone in Baghdad controlled by coalition forces during Operation Iraqi Freedom.

The edifice appeared completely unassuming with a plain facade on which a single door and no windows faced the street. No words were painted on the outer walls, nor did any signs hang at the entrance. In fact, it was seldom if ever that an occasion arose when someone actually arrived at the front entrance and used that door. Everyone in the *Zona Verde* knew just who controlled that building, and absolutely no one asked just what it was that people did there.

Like most of the people who approached that building with intent and confidence, *Capitán* and his entourage arrived at the back side of the building and entered through a door hidden from the view of the street. As they entered, they were confronted by a maze of shelves standing twenty-five feet tall lined with boxes of unknown content, computer mainframes in sections, personal computers in various conditions from disassembled to boxed and seemingly ready to ship to retailers. There were also computer monitors, television sets, and all manner of other electronic devices, which also appeared new as they were in their boxes. Had it been an unfamiliar visitor to the premises looking at this poorly lit labyrinth of appliances, they would have been completely stunted in their step. But *Capitán* was very well acquainted with the site and its functions, which were varied.

He led his men down one path that took them to the farthest wall from the back entrance, where they came upon an elevator which they entered. Although the elevator push button pad told of only one subterranean floor, *Capitán inserted* a key into the keyhole right next to it and turned it prompting the elevator doors to close, taking them down two floors to a secret bunker. As the elevator doors opened, the men proceeded to enter into an immense office and lab area, which was so brightly lit that for a moment *Capitán* and his group of four tough, macho henchmen found themselves squinting hard as their delicate pupils suffered a mild case of photophobia due to light sensitivity.

They rubbed their eyelids and dried off tears as they readjusted their vision to see that there were men and women young and old interacting in their various see-through, glass-walled offices and laboratories. Most of them wore white lab coats and scrubs that made them all appear exceptionally clean and sterile. A huge contrast to the rag-tag bunch wearing cowboy boots, black and blue denim pants, (at least two of whom wore a leather vest, and the ever-present cowboy hat) that had just unloaded themselves from the elevator. Yet, although they appeared to be completely out of their natural habitat and, therefore, not belonging there, no one even looked in the direction of the men.

For *Capitán*, who was accustomed to it, none of this was new or surprising. Yet his men had never been allowed down there. For them this was a first, and they looked like Alice in Wonderland after falling through the rabbit hole to discover a hidden world. They followed *Capitán* as he led them past the various glass-walled offices until they came upon a *mahogany* door. Without hesitation, their leader barged through that door startling the lone occupant, who jumped up from behind a table cluttered with a laptop, papers, a lamp, a desktop computer, headphones, and another stack of papers and manila folders. *Capitán* turned around to face his crew stopping them in their tracks before they could follow him inside. He instructed them to stand guard at the door and let no one come near for a five-foot radius. The men, with their machine guns held firmly, nodded at their leader and assumed the position of guards as *Capitán* shut the door.

Once inside, *Capitán* approached the cluttered workspace where a nervous, young man wearing bifocals, a black t-shirt, jeans, and sneakers, which contrasted greatly with the serious-looking white lab coat he wore on top of it all, stood wringing his hands.

"I... I wasn't expecting you back so soon," said the young man hesitantly.

"What have you learned from the footage?" replied *Capitán* getting straight down to business.

"Not a whole lot, actually. But some significant information."

"Show me."

"Well," the young man said, motioning with his hands an invitation at *Capitán* to come around the table and see what he was about to show him on the screen of his laptop. *Capitán* remained solidly in place, staring at him. The young man acknowledged the tacit directive and simply flipped the laptop around for *Capitán* to get a clear view.

"...it took me hours to find anything on him. I searched endlessly. This guy was a tough cookie to find. But through some sources of mine—"

"I don't need all the details of your search. Just give me the meat of it. Who the hell is this guy?"

"The reality is that he seems to have come out of nowhere. There's no record of him longer than just a few months, so it's impossible to know who he really is, but I think that guy who shot up the bus station is the same guy who's been shooting up places in Texas, too."

"How do you know this is the same man?" *Capitán* inquired.

"Well, the string of incidents in Texas are identical to what happened here. The man in Texas shot the TV sets while a *novela* was playing, and the description given by some witnesses match quite perfectly the man on the video you brought from the bus station."

"I see. What else do you know?"

"Not much else, I'm sorry to say. Like I said before, it's like this guy just popped out of nowhere. As if he was conjured up from another realm."

"Believe me, he's no supernatural being. He's a man…but not just any man. This guy could be just what we've been looking for to advance our plans for the future of this organization. It is imperative that we get to him first before anyone else finds him."

"Um, let me see…" the young man said as he looked around the room seemingly searching the walls and the floor for more information to satiate his superior's demands. "Oh, I got it! I can tell you where he's going."

"Okay. Out with it."

"As I said before, he's been cited in different cities in Texas and now he's here. So, that's gotta mean that he's on a predetermined course southbound. He shot up the bus station, which tells me that he had a reason to be there. He's not driving, he's using public transportation. So, he's got to be on board one of those buses heading into the interior. Exactly where he's headed is hard to say but there is a finite number of destinations. If you could question some of the people at the bus station about this guy using the footage and descriptions we have of him, I'm sure you'll be able to find the exact route."

Capitán took a moment to ponder the findings, rubbing his chin as he contemplated the information. He looked at the young man after some time and let a slight smirk rise on his lips giving him a sign of approval.

"Good work. Keep it up. When the time comes for us to rise, you will have a proper place at the table. I've taken all measures to convince *Comander* that you have been dealt with. He believes that you are dead. That's why I placed you here in this bunker with a new identity. Just stick to the plan exactly as I've laid it out. If you are found out, we are both dead men. If that happens, the worse thing would not be getting killed but the way that *Comander* would do it. So, lay low and talk to no one about what we've discussed here. Even those workers outside your door. I know they have no contact with the boss, but still… No one is to be trusted. Soon we will make our move. I'm sure you have seen the reports of ashfall throughout the country?"

The young man seemed thrown off by the sudden shift in *Capitán's* discourse.

"Um, yes. I have."

"People wonder where it's coming from or what it means," continued *Capitán,* without acknowledging the young man's input. "But I have no doubts… It's a potent sign. Remember the code of the Order of the Jaguar Knights: from the ashes of an apparent defeat we shall strike with the jaws of victory!"

****

Chapter 4
"ON THE ROAD"

Marco stared intently at the sun's last gleaming watching it nearing the edge of the horizon as he rested his head on the window of his seat in the bus. With a quick eye gesture, he'd cleared the aisle seat of a man who had tried to take it. Marco's look told the stranger to take a hike and look for a seat elsewhere. He was consumed by deep thoughts of his past. A past he had relinquished not too long ago when he had changed his identity to erase all links that could lead back to people he cared about. It was a means to protect them from forces which were, no doubt, still on his trail, and who could harm anyone close to him in order to push him out of the shadows. As he focused more and more on the events of his past, his eyes became like inverted cameras that turned their focus from the view of the sunset inward to his memories as he slid into a lucid dream.

It was the day of the U.S. presidential inaugural address. Marco had been assigned to cover the reaction of the losing campaign. He was to spend the day with the then ex-presidential candidate Carmine Hilton. After the address, the Hilton camp headed back to his estate with Marco following along. At the residence, they finally had a chance to sit down and discuss the day's events in view of the entire presidential run. He had blamed many things as the cause of his loss but kept coming back to a seemingly insignificant event that had occurred well into the race close to election day. He had referred to his opponent's supporters as "a batch of depreciables" because of the nature of their rhetoric which was increasingly divisive and dismissive of traditional democratic norms. Marco noticed he was intent on talking about the incident and the meaning he had intended.

"You know, Marco," Mr. Hilton said, "I never meant to say that Americans who supported my opponent were depreciable themselves. I meant it in the sense that when we let ourselves get carried away by negative emotions, we diminish the value of our national discourse and over time that can only bring negative consequences. Of course, the opposition didn't bother to take the full context of my words into account and they just pounced on the apparent meaning, making me look like I thought less of his supporters. And the media didn't help. They, too, jumped on the sensational aspect of the story and painted a terrible picture of me and my campaign. As if my opponent and his supporters in government and in other circles needed any more ammunition with which to demonize me."

Marco looked intently at Mr. Hilton as he tried to clean up his own mess. It was clear he was being especially nice and welcoming to him at his residential headquarters because he wanted Marco's assistance in polishing his political image. The curious thing to Marco was why Mr. Hilton wanted that. He had made it known in other interviews that he did not intend to run for political office again after that major defeat. Yet his demeanor and the great effort to whitewash his own words by explaining their intended meaning was a clear sign that Mr. Hilton wanted to, at the very least, leave the door open to the possibility of a comeback at some point in the future. All his efforts were clearly him maneuvering to cast himself in better light. Marco knew Mr. Hilton had no one else to blame but himself for the ghastly slipups throughout his campaign, which didn't exactly cost him the presidency in and of themselves, but they sure didn't help him in any way. But Marco was a sensitive man. He did not want to press the defeated presidential candidate. Not on that day especially. He sympathized with him. He had spoken words of support for minorities of all kinds. He exemplified, in Marco's view, the ideal Democratic political leader who supported inclusion and equality. And above all else, since Marco's roots stemmed back to Central America, he was especially fond of Mr. Hilton because he had spoken in defense of the refugees on the border who had become a giant political piñata for the opposition's increasingly race-baiting, nationalistic rhetoric.

Mr. Hilton's opponent had run on the promise to eliminate the "illegal immigrant problem" once and for all. Once, on a press conference, he had hinted at the need to use extreme measures that could deliver a "solution that is final". Of course, many people in the media, in sports, celebrities, political figures and the public at large were outraged at the apparent demagoguery and clear insensitivity to immigrants a statement like that represented, since it was uncomfortably similar to the Nazis' "final solution" to the "Jewish question". Nevertheless, he had won the presidency, albeit by a very slim margin. Marco observed Mr. Hilton as he seemed to go on and off into quiet spells. His eyes glossing over as if he were immersed in flight, watching from above the events that had led to this solemn moment of reevaluation in the face of defeat.

For once in a very long time, Marco didn't see himself as a hungry reporter out to get the scoop to score points and climb the ladder in investigative reporting. He saw himself as a supporter, who himself, was struggling with the reality of his candidate's loss. For that reason, he let his interviewee determine the shape of his final report, which he delivered that very night of the inaugural address.

Days later Marco found himself in a very different world when he returned to The Daily News Report's central office to find that his own desk had been reassigned to another reporter.

"Excuse me, you made a mistake. This is my office. That's my chair you're sitting in," Marco said from the entrance to the man who was seemingly disinterested in his input.

"Not anymore," the reporter responded without even looking at Marco.

"Seriously, what are you doing here? This is my workspace, everyone knows that."

"I told you. It isn't anymore. You have a problem with that? Talk to the boss upstairs."

"Huh?" Marco still couldn't grasp the situation. He remained at the door staring at the reporter usurping his desk until, with great disdain, the reporter breathed deeply and exhaled loudly to signal his displeasure at being interrupted, but he finally turned to Marco acknowledging his presence.

"Look, buddy. Yes, everyone knows this WAS your desk, okay? But it isn't anymore. Didn't you get the memo?" He turned to his desk flipping through stacks and stacks of papers until he came upon a sheet.

"Here, I even printed it out just in case. I should have posted it on the door. You can have it. Now, if you could please find it in yourself to get out of my face and let me get back to work, I would really treasure that. Okay? Thanks." The reporter winked at Marco as he dismissed him sarcastically, quickly turning back to his work as if Marco had suddenly disappeared.

As for Marco, it took a few more instances to let the reality of the situation filter through until he understood what had happened. The memo had clearly come from upstairs and stated that Marco's office would go to the other reporter. In it was also Marco's new assignment. Essentially, he had been demoted from investigative reporter back to beat reporter, having been assigned that year's main street parade. He fumed at the thought of having been demoted in such an embarrassing manner. He headed straight to the boss's office at the top floor and barged right in, circumventing the receptionist, who tried to hold him back urging him to stop.

"It's okay, Ofelia. It's okay. Let him through," said Laurie Gow, News Editor for The Daily News Report.

"What's the meaning of this?" Asked Marco holding up the memo in his hand.

"Marco, what is the nature of an investigative reporter's job in your view?"

Marco stood still, unsure where she was going with that question.

"I'll tell you what it isn't," Laurie added. "It isn't that report you sent me of your interview with Mr. Hilton."

"I don't understand. I thought you wanted me to cover Mr. Hilton's reactions and overall feelings about the election results. That's exactly what I did."

"Maybe to some degree. But we are in the business of news here, Marco. I need you to find news for me. That requires a gutsy attitude and a take-no-prisoners mentality. What you gave me was a report based on a series of softball questions that shed no new light into the national discourse. How do you think this will reflect on my paper? You cost me a front-page news lead. That, I cannot forgive."

"So, you immediately give my office away to another reporter and put me on the beat? I've proved myself to you many times. It's why you promoted me to lead investigative reporter, Laurie. Where is all this coming from?"

"I think you got a little too emotionally invested in this story and you let it affect your judgment. So, as a friendly reminder of what your task is, I put you back on the beat as a temporary admonishment. C'mon, Marco. You knew better than to send me something that I was going to have to send to the back end of the paper. You're better than that. You're not just a reporter, you're an investigative journalist. Act like one. This demotion will help you regain your perspective and your hunger for real reporting."

Marco stood silently looking at Laurie's desktop turning over her words in his head. He knew she was right. He had given the ex-presidential candidate a pass. Besides, he thought perhaps this new arrangement could help him gain a better appreciation for his work and the value of his reporting.

"Marco, I have always had great faith in you. Which is why this is only a temporary deal. Go out there and put your nose to the grindstone. Work hard and soon enough you'll be back where you belong. By the

way, you do know that the president-elect has secretly commissioned a team to explore possibilities for his 'solution' to the illegal immigrant 'problem' right?"
Laurie stated in air quotes, as she shifted in her chair.

Marco turned his eyes back up looking straight at Laurie.

"Conjecture, so far as anyone knows," he responded.

"Well, I'm not so sure. But then again, it takes some serious investigating on behalf of capable individuals in the press to find out the truth. See why I acted on you like I did? I'm telling you this in confidence. In all my team there is no one else that I think is capable of getting to the bottom of a story like this one other than you. That is why I need you to be on your very best. Get this beat story done and play it cool and then I will back you one hundred percent with whatever you need to do what you do best: breaking real news. In the meantime, everyone here needs to see that I do not tolerate the slightest sluggishness from even my best reporters. It's the only way to stay ahead of the game, my friend."

"I understand," said Marco after a brief moment, finally realizing that the gesture was not entirely a slight against him but more of an act of self-

preservation for an organization involved in a highly competitive industry, which could easily go bankrupt if its workers failed to produce high-quality products.

"What about my office? Where will I be working from?" asked Marco before stepping out of his boss's office.

"That's the least of your worries. It's not the office that makes the reporter, it's the size of his bite. Find any table in the staff commons area and get to work," she replied finally dismissing him.

On the day of the parade, Marco stood among the crowd of expectant observers watching the approaching procession led by high school cheerleading squads performing cartwheels and other acrobatics. They twirled batons, tossing them in the air as they gave a quick spin on their heels and catching the batons without breaking step. Following the youngsters were a series of floats carrying all manner of cartoonish decorations and hauling large inflated balloons reaching several stories high matching the height of a few of the buildings along the street, though most were much taller skyscrapers that stood way out of reach. The crowds on the sidewalks were following the procession, which is why Marco noticed that suddenly he was packed tightly in a sea of humanity. He began to move counter-current, since he wanted to escape the tuna-can grip of the front end of the mob. It took him a while to come to a clearing near the end of the procession. All the while he had been struggling to find the "angle" with which to cover the, otherwise, boring event. He clearly was not a fan of such gatherings. So, it was extremely difficult for him to find some interesting take with which to cover the story. He knew that this one had to be not only news-worthy and entertaining to the paper's audience, but it would especially have to be interesting and newsworthy to his boss, Laurie Gow.

The next occurrence as he meditated in search of a story was like a scene out of a romantic comedy. As a big group of people approaching him broke apart to circle past him, a large gap opened to reveal the sight of an angel in his eyes. There she stood in full radiance. A creature of unparalleled physical beauty and a countenance which transmitted the confidence of a goddess. She was tall, brown skinned, light brown hair, hazel eyes and a figure that would make 1950s pinup models envious in her long, form-fitting dress. He could not believe his eyes, and his luck. Who would have thought that after so many years he could be standing face to face again with the one and only woman whom he'd ever truly loved?

"Marco?" she asked similarly in disbelief.

"Sally..."

"Oh my god, it really is you!" She ran and jumped into his arms, and as if preprogramed by some mechanism that governs romantic reencounters, he lifted her in the air, spinning her around 180-degrees, until he put her back on her feet on the opposite side.

"I can't believe this. What are you doing here!?"

"Uh, working. But I should be asking you that! What brings you to the city? When did you get here," he asked, since it was she, in fact, the one who was visiting.

"Me too. Working."

"Still covering events, then?"

"Yep. Got my own column now, though. No more freelancing."

"Oh, congratulations!"

"Thank you."

"So how do you like it?" said Marco.

"It's a pretty nice gig, you know. I wouldn't trade it for anything. I get to pick most of my stories and, obviously, get to travel."

"My god, how long has it been?"

"Ugh, years! Too long, really," she responded quickly adding more to change the topic. "What about you? What have you been up to? I've read some of your work on the paper."

"You have?"

"Yeah, once in a while." She tried to downplay the fact that she still kept a watch on at least his professional activities.

"Well, I had been promoted to lead investigative reporter at the Daily, but..." He paused and looked away.

"But what?" She asked.

"But this. I'm here, ain't I?" He giggled and she joined in not quite sure what to make of his comment.

"You mean they got you covering this event?"

"That's right. They tossed me right back down the ladder to beat reporter."

"That's awful. I'm sorry to hear that. Why did they do that? I don't understand. Just recently I saw your very latest piece on the Hilton presidential campaign. I thought it was great."

"You're too nice. Unfortunately, my boss wasn't too happy with it, and so here I am."

"Well, I think that's terrible."

"No. It isn't," Marco replied appearing to stop time with his eyes as his pupils focused intently on hers for the first time in ages.

"It isn't?" She was awestruck as she returned the gaze into his eyes, feeling like she was at the beginning of a plunge into a deep well. Suddenly all the memories of the past came surging from deep inside her, paralyzing her in mid speech, her mouth agape as if she were a fish out of water.

He, too, found himself amid an emotional earthquake emanating from deep within the pit of his stomach. The feeling was such that he felt his lungs collapsing, blocking his tubes as he struggled to breath. All the while his heart thumped louder and louder in his ears canceling out all the chatter, music, and sounds of the parade. Somehow, he managed to put one foot in front of the other and moved himself closer to Sally.

"It isn't... Because it brought me back to you..."

The loud screeching of breaks on the second-class bus ripped through the cabin, waking all the travelers as the interior lamps turned on. Marco came out of his reverie just as he was about to relive a moment he had not remembered for a long time. He didn't even remember if he had kissed Sally on that day of the parade almost a year ago. He had allowed the feeling of happiness to return because he was reliving the moment as if for the very first time again. However, this abrupt stop in the middle of nowhere on a dark Mexican night forced him to relinquish his thoughts of love and focus on what was happening in the moment. He knew what it could be. An arbitrary checkpoint set up by either federal police or the military. He hoped it wouldn't be something else, like an arbitrary checkpoint by men impersonating federal police or the military. All would become crystal clear as soon as the men boarded the bus, depending on what they asked of the travelers.

For his part, Marco was ready for anything. He had been in similar situations before, so he knew how to act around cops and military personnel in Mexico. But their impersonators were a different story. They could kidnap them and ask for ransoms or execute them on the spot. Whatever was coming, Marco had a quick solution for either scenario. On one hand, he had a few bills of cash to pay his way past the roadblock. On the other, he caressed the butt of his revolver ready to pull it out and go down in a steady stream of gunfire. Of course, he would stand no chance against the military men, who carried their fearsome FX-05 Xiuhcoatl, the Mexican military's "Fire Serpent".

As if prognosticated by Marco's thoughts, a short, dark-skinned, young man dressed in military garb and carrying a heavy-looking Xihucoatl (which appeared to surpass in length what the soldier measured in height), entered the bus. He was followed by another man of identical description. The only distinction between the two was that the first one, who had begun to ask passengers for documents and the nature of their travel, was a slim, athletic-looking young man. Whereas his companion guarding the door was an older, more frail-looking fellow, though his eyes transmitted an equal degree of mortal consequence to anyone who would challenge him.

When the young Mexican soldier reached him, Marco had made up his mind that these were not outlaws, but official representatives of the Mexican military. Therefore, he put his gun away in his backpack and quickly placed it under the seat in front of him. He had determined that he would hand the soldier his money, as he was sure to be asked for a bribe. This wasn't in a mistaken expectation of normalcy and due process. He was well aware that even official representatives of the government could extort people traveling through the country.

"Identification," said the soldier dryly. Marco showed him his professionally made fake Id. which so far had served him well with no issues.

"Ticket," demanded the soldier, as well. "Where are you headed?"

"*Ciudad de Mexico,* replied Marco.

"What's your business in our capital?"

"Visiting family, *patron*." Marco used the deferential term "*patron*" which was the common term of respect for someone in a position of authority in the northern region of Mexico.

The soldier looked at him squarely in the eyes, in spite of the fact that Marco towered over him. Nonetheless, the soldier was fearless. And though he carried the Fire Serpent on his right arm, leaning it against his chest and over his shoulder, like a father carrying an over-grown son or daughter, it was clear by the fury in his eyes that he would just as easily dispense of a man of Marco's size with his bare hands.

To Marco's surprise, the soldier handed him all his documents without further question and proceeded to the next passenger. He mulled over the question of voluntarily offering the soldier the cash he had on-hand, but he opted not to stir the pot any more than was needed. He sat back down instead and waited to see what their next move would be. This, too, was a surprise, because the soldier sped up the rest of the inspection and quickly exited the bus. Soon, everyone was breathing easy again, starting to slouch back into their seats, as the driver pulled the bus back onto the isolated freeway dimly lit solely by the light of the full moon. With the steady hum of the engine rocking everyone into a lull, Marco himself succumbed once again to sleep, where he returned to his past life.

On the eve of the publication of his piece exposing the president's secret panel tasked with exploring possible solutions to the illegal immigrant problem, Marco had made plans to meet with Sally for the first time after their reencounter to have dinner and talk. She had insisted that they take it slow, not labeling anything. It wouldn't be a date, so much as just two friends hanging out. Marco was fine with that arrangement mainly for the same reasons they had grown apart in their previous life together: he was just too busy to play the committed boyfriend.

He was finishing up getting dressed in his apartment about to head to the door when he received a text notification. It was her. Just wanted to let him know she was on her way to the restaurant. Don't be late as usual!

"Good things come to those who wait. I'll see you in a bit," he replied with winking, smiling face emojis.

Marco put away his phone in his pocket and shut off the lights. As he was about to open the door, the phone rang. He thought it might be Sally calling, having perhaps not seen his response to her text. It was his boss, Laurie.

"Have you seen the news today?" said Laurie over the phone.

"No, why? What's going on?"

"Not much, if you consider that it's a story about an immigrant child found dead on the side of a highway. Just another tragic consequence of risking your life for liberty, right?"

"So, I suppose there's a lot more to it than just the run-of-the-mill homicide?" Marco paused, curious as to why this story in the news had prompted Laurie to call him about it. This was usually something that happened when there was a real scoop and she wanted him to get on it. But, so far, he wasn't seeing the angle.

"Well, I would have just mindlessly carried on with my TV programming like any regular Joe on a Saturday night. But something stuck out that I think might interest you. By the way, I want to congratulate you again on the first part of your piece on the president's immigrant panel. But, given that the work is still in progress, how is that going? You know we'll need to move very fast with this exposé."

"It's going. I have a few sources inside the White House who've given me some good leads. Apparently, there is some sort of plan for construction of centers for immigrants—" before he finished his sentence, Laurie interjected.

"They've already been building those detention centers for years now. What's new about that?" she asked.

"No, not detention centers. A different kind of center. The tip was vague. My informant also doesn't really know the full details, but he's working on getting more info to me soon."

Marco paused momentarily, wondering where the conversation was headed. He was trying to piece together Laurie's mention of the dead immigrant child's case with his investigation.

"So, what does this have to do with the story you mentioned?"

"Other than that it's about an immigrant who was raped and murdered in our country in this age of anti-immigrants? Not much. Unless you take into account the fact that the child's body was completely covered in ashes. Why? No one can tell. The police have no suspects and no clue why the body was covered in ashes like that."

"I gotta be honest, boss. I still don't see the connection. Sounds like it could be a completely random act of violence, doesn't it?" asked Marco.

"Sure. But what I can't stop wondering about is the ash, Marco. What was this little girl doing covered in ashes? Dirt, I get it. Filth, sure. But ashes? Why?"

"Maybe it was some sort of ritualistic killing. Some weird satanic cult might have gotten a hold of the poor little girl and covered her up in ashes as a symbolic offering or something."

"That's pretty good guessing. But that's not what gets you back to the top, Marco."

"What are you saying?" asked Marco fearing what he suspected coming from his boss.

"I'm saying that I want you to put off whatever plans you had for tonight and go dig up everything you can about this girl's case. I really think there's more to it than just a simple case of ritualistic killing. Who knows, it could be tied to the government's immigrant solution. I say that because of reports of ash falling seemingly out of nowhere in several towns in the Midwest. Nobody knows where it's coming from. It seems it only falls at night."

"Yeah, I've seen the reports. It's quite interesting," said Marco. He was conflicted thinking that he couldn't just put off this story, but at the same time he didn't want to have to cancel on Sally. Not after having gone without her company for so long. She had accepted his invitation and now he would be standing her up. This would not have good results for his goal of getting back together with her.

"Marco are you there?" asked Laurie.

"Yes. Sorry, I was just thinking about what I'm going to say to the person I was going to meet tonight. It's not going to go over too well."

"Just tell that person the truth, Marco. That you are being forced by your bitch of a boss to drop everything you had planned tonight and go work on a story."

"Right," answered Marco feigning amusement at Laurie's attempted humor.

A full two weeks had passed since their botched friendly date. Sally had not returned any of his calls, nor had she texted him back. He had been secretly "stalking" her social media profiles, but even those seemed ignored by her. The most recent update on one of her profiles was from six months before. It was a picture of herself with a local celebrity at a fundraiser. Marco was beginning to think that this time she meant to stay clear of him, even on chance meetings in public. Perhaps, he thought, it would be better to end it before it even started again. He tended to think of relationships as milk, telling his friends,

"... once it goes bad, you can't use it on your cereal anymore. Unless you like cereal with the taste of decay."

One night, Marco found himself at the White House Correspondent's Dinner at the capital. He was there primarily at the behest of his editor, who thought it a perfect opportunity to gauge the political world's response to the growing evidence uncovered through his investigative reporting on the president's secret immigrant panel. Marco complied more so because of the off chance that he could run into Sally again, than because of his boss's insistence. After all, the man at the center of his investigative reporting was going to be speaking there only a few feet away and happened to be the most powerful man in the world. Of course, Marco did not plan to stay for that, and risk being scrutinized directly or be the pun of what would feel like inappropriate jokes given the circumstances.

He made a few rounds by Laurie's side as she attempted to introduce him to senators and other political heavy hitters. He tried to partake in the banter, but Washington bred a whole different set of animals. Even other reporters and correspondents seemed strange and distant. Marco felt like he had been abducted and thrown into a gathering of aliens. They were, for the most part, a pale-skinned, seemingly cold-hearted and crass bunch walking around on stilts, it seemed, since they towered over Marco. They joked about poverty, the liberal left, the far right, immigration, and deportation (off the record, of course) like those things were just items to nibble on in a dish of word Hors d'oeuvres from which they were completely detached. The uneasiness got to him so badly that on the first distraction he attempted to slip away unsuspectedly, but Laurie caught him by the arm before he did so.

"I got some bad news, kid," said Laurie in as maternal a tone as she could manage. "We're going to

have to pull the plug on your investigation into the government's immigrant panel."

"What? Why?"

"The House of Representatives is forming a special committee to look into human rights violations against immigrants by the administration. I've been asked to scale it back a bit on the coverage...actually, a lot. They want us off the story," Laurie said, for the first time sounding as if she were just another of his co-workers taking orders from a higher up.

"Scale it back? I'm on the brink of busting this thing wide open, Laurie. This could be huge!"

"I know, Marco. That's why we need to tone it down. You think your coverage hasn't perked up ears and raised eyebrows among these guys? That's why they came to me. It's getting too hot."

"Laurie, I don't know what to say to you. You were the one pushing me to go out there and do what I do best. Now you're killing my story?"

"Not me. There are bigger forces on this than you and me, and the paper, Marco. What do you think will happen if you do end up cracking this case wide open and exposing everything that's going on and everyone involved? You think you'll be given a medal of recognition for it? We don't know how big this thing is. And for me to have had these folks secretly approach me to tell me—not ask, but tell me—that I need to quash it? Well, I don't know about you, but I intend to have a

career for a while. We have done all we could on this. Don't look so disappointed, Marco. You've done very well. It's because of your work that we have moved these people to take some sort of action and look into it. Our work is done...for now."

"I've sacrificed a lot for this story. I have worked so much. What am I going to tell my sources inside? Thank you, have a nice life? They're going to come after them sooner or later, Laurie."

"I know, Marco. We both know what this job is all about. Sources know what they are getting into when they decide to help us out. It's the nature of it. Even if you continued on the story, what do you think you could do for them if or when they got caught leaking to the press? You're just a journalist, Marco. A damn good one, but still just a journalist. You can't protect them. And at this juncture, I want you to have some possibility of protecting yourself by distancing yourself from it. You know damn well that in this era of 'fake news' and social media guys like us, our paper, we don't stand a chance. We'd be shut down fast. We have to learn when to hold 'em and when to fold 'em, my friend."

"These politicians aren't going to do shit about it, and you know it!"

"Yeah, well..." said Laurie exasperated. "neither are we!"

Laurie took one last look sternly into Marco's eyes and ended the conversation by tapping him on the shoulder and walking away before he could muster a retort.

Marco stood there watching Laurie get back to the crowd of Washington elites. He was seething with rage. He had always looked up to Laurie. Whether in good times or bad. When she praised him and when she admonished him. She was consistently a person of virtue and principle in his eyes. But at that very moment, he saw her as no different than all those politicians slithering around each other like snakes, smiling fake smiles and exchanging pleasantries grounded on the flimsiest of genuine intentions.

As Marco headed toward the exit, his angel appeared before him once again through the doors at the entrance. Sally stood there radiating her sparkling eyes at him. The world came to a standstill. His jaw dropped as he searched for words. Should he start with "Hello," or go straight into "I'm sorry I stood you up," he could not decide. Marco broke the spell if only temporarily to grab Sally by the hand and, without saying a thing, lead her away from the crowd toward a balcony where they could talk.

Outside, standing in the cold night on the balcony, a secret service agent stood on a far corner watching them intently as they made their way to the rail. Sally shivered. He took off his jacket, and though he felt the immediate shock of the chill on his back, Marco felt gratified that she did not refuse his gesture. He felt like he was hugging her by putting his coat on her shoulders, and she was enjoying his embrace.

"Sally, I'm so sorry for what happened the last time..."

"It's okay. I know you're a busy guy. I'm quite busy myself. Which is why I had not been able to respond to your messages. Don't think I hadn't noticed."

"I thought you were angry and just ignoring me."

"Well, I wasn't elated. But then I thought about things and the reality is, we can't keep doing this to each other, Marco.

We have to move on. We tried this once. It didn't work. Maybe it was a sign."

"Look, I'm not trying to change your mind. But I really feel like this was just a bad coincidence. I really felt like we were onto something this time around. Who knows? Maybe this time is for keeps."

"Marco, please—"

"Just let me explain, okay? Two minutes and then we go back inside to the warmth."

She looked at him, tightened his jacket around herself to shield from the frigid air, and looked out into the distance giving him space to speak.

"I know this is going to sound crazy, but there is something really strange happening. That night we were going to meet up, I..." he stopped mid-sentence noticing her facial expression as it changed somewhat. Her eyes *were focused on a specific thing he could not see. It was clear by the look on her face that her attention was on something other than him and his confession.*

"What is it?" he asked trying not to sound hurt at the thought of being ignored when he was attempting to open up to her.

"Look," Sally pointed to the sky.

At first, he could not tell what she was pointing at. It was a combination of the bright lights from below and the black sky in the background that prevented him from seeing clearly. But then, out of the darkness, a flurry of tiny debris appeared floating down toward them. It looked like the initial stages of snow fall. But these tiny objects were nothing like snowflakes. They were greyish. Almost like ash. Marco stuck out his hand. As he saw a few flakes landing on his palm he retrieved it to inspect them closely. Since the poor lighting did not help in that endeavor he instinctively resorted to the time-tested method of human study of the world: he licked the flakes off his hand. The taste was a bit salty with a hint of oak or hickory. Sally and Marco looked at each other equally perplexed. No one had ever seen grey flakes—ash, that is—falling on the white house since probably the 1800s. Something was burning profusely somewhere in the capital.

Sally turned to him abruptly and said,

"I got to get back inside. We'll talk later, ok?"

"Sally, wait," he said, wanting desperately to tell her what he had been bottling up for so long. That he needed her. That he wanted her and couldn't stand losing her again.

"Marco, it's not the time right now. But we'll talk. I promise," she said as she was taking his coat off. Something about the weight of the garment seemed strange. Sally had stretched her arm to hand him the coat but then retrieved it and pressed it against her body feeling around for something that was clearly adding weight to it. She put her hand in a pocket and pulled out a small .22 pistol.

"What's this? she demanded.

"Oh, actually," he responded quickly taking the gun and the coat from her hands to conceal the weapon from the secret service.

"How did you get that in here, Marco? What's it for?"

"Look, Sally. It's complicated. But there is a very good explanation. See, I've been getting some anonymous threats lately, because of the story I've been working on. Nothing serious, I'm sure. But, still. I thought I should be ready for anything, you know?"

Sally looked at him as if she hardly knew him. He had always been full of surprises, but she never would have thought that he'd be the type to carry a gun.

"Marco, whatever is going on, you need to be careful and take good care of yourself." He saw something in her eyes that he'd never seen before. It was a slight sense of pity mixed with uncertainty. She could just have been talking about him being careful out there in the world given the death threats. But he knew she also meant for him to check his mental state.

"It's not like that," he said.

The look in Sally's eyes softened once again.

"I have to go now," she said, walking away from him.

"Sir, we're with the FBI. You need to come with us," a voice startled Marco as he was standing there on the balcony looking at Sally enter back into the building.

"If this is about the gun, I can explain. I do have a permit."

"No, sir. It's not about the gun, but you do have to hand it over," said one of the FBI agents extending his hand. They took Marco behind the building and used a staircase that led them down to the ground floor where a car sitting idly waited for them to board.

****

Chapter 5
"SLEEPY TOWN, U.M.S.
(UNITED MEXICAN STATES)"

The light bulb flickered continuously as it swayed back and forth from the ceiling of the covered parking area for arrivals at the bus terminal in the city of San Luis Potosi, in the state of San Luis Potosi, on the way to Mexico City, in the state of Mexico, in Mexico. An elderly man sat motionlessly on a plastic patio chair looking like a docile gargoyle with his hand held out supported by his elbow which rested on his flat gut. His palm faced up as he remained poised between the two doors right outside of the men and women's restrooms. Any other foreigner might have thought him to be some street performer acting like a statue for the public's entertainment and for a possible charitable collection, but Marco quickly recognized him as a beggar looking for spare change.

Marco sat still in his seat on the bus for a few moments after waking from his dream of the past. His hands still felt Sally's presence as if he had just moments before let go of her soft, warm hand in the cold Washington night. Marco had considered fully disclosing to her what he planned to do. He would change his name. Fake his own death and go underground. Marco knew she would understand, since this would be for a cause like no other. Akin to saving the world in a way. But he realized that if he brought her into it, he would be compromising her safety. It was necessary to cut off all ties. No matter how hard it would be or how much it would hurt. And this was certain to hurt not only him. He was sure to break her heart forever. His faked death would mean Marco could never come back into Sally's life to reveal the ruse.

He took one more moment to remember Sally's love, and just like a TV set, he shut off his brain's image feed bringing his awareness fully to his surroundings. Marco turned his attention once more to see the old man through window and made his way straight to him as he exited the vehicle. The closer he got to the man the more he noticed a blue hue lightly glowing on the old man's features in the night. Marco realized it was a small, hand-held TV/Radio device the man had in his non-begging hand. As he came within inches of the man, Marco pulled out a few dollar bills from the small pocket in his blue jeans. He didn't count it, although he knew it couldn't be more than five dollars in ones. But when he paid notice to the sound and images that came from the hand-held TV, he put the brakes on his intended generosity to ask some questions of the man in the chair.

"Is there nothing else a man could be doing while asking for donations than to sit around watching *novelas*?"

"It is all there is on this channel," responded the old man laboriously through crooked and gapped teeth.

"Surely you could simply change the channel, couldn't you?"

"I don't know how to do that."

Marco looked the man in the eyes pondering the seemingly ridiculous notion that he, or anyone for that matter, could not operate a simple, outmoded device. But the old man's eyes spoke clear truth even though they were lightly glazed over with what looked like white melted sugar. The man was honestly ignorant as to how to change channels on his TV.

"What about asking someone to help you with that? Don't you have family? Someone helping you out."

"Sometimes my daughter comes by and checks up on me. But she hasn't been around all night. I don't know where she is. I had to go to the restroom earlier, but since I am crippled, I couldn't get up so, I just went here. I guess people simply come to a point where they just become a burden on others around them. There is nothing else for me to look forward to in this world but death."

Marco's initial scorn at the man watching *novelas* while begging for money from strangers changed instantly to deep sympathy because now, he had been reminded of his own deceased grandfather. His grandfather had confessed to feeling like a burden on his family since he lost his mobility and required adult diapers, which his own daughters and his son would reluctantly take turns changing, though not without first arguing and fighting over having to do it at all.

The old man's eyes had begun to tear up as he told Marco that he had soiled himself. Marco turned his attention briefly away from the man to look around. No one was there other than those who had arrived with him in the bus. He turned back to the old man who still held his begging hand up in place throughout the entire conversation. For that commitment Marco rewarded the old man with the bills he'd pulled out from his pocket. The old man thanked him with great appreciation through light sobs of self-pity. Marco felt a great rush of emotions which he momentarily did not know how to express. Those feelings were like he either wanted to hug the man tightly like he was his beloved grandfather or kick someone to death for condemning this poor man to such misery. Quite suddenly the matter was resolved in Marco's head without giving a hint to anyone of the emotional debate that had gripped him.

"Where do you think I could find your daughter, *abuelo*? Is she close by? I need to ask her for a favor."

"She is usually home tending to her matters, watching her *novelas*." The old man had pointed to a small shanty across the parking lot of the bus station. Marco took the TV/Radio and turned the dial until he saw a black and white movie from the Mexican Golden Era of film. It was *Tin-Tan* in "*El Rey del Barrio*".

"Here, watch this. You will never lose as many brain cells with this story as with those horrendous *novelas*. Take care of yourself, *abue*. Things are going to get better. You'll see."

Marco turned and sprinted away from the old man. He approached the bus driver who had scurried all the passengers back onto the bus and was about to depart. Marco asked him for a brief delay. The driver, of course, said "absolutely not". Marco pulled a twenty-dollar bill and asked for five minutes. The driver smiled and nodded saying "With pleasure, *caballero*."

Marco ran out toward the house the old man had pointed to. The windows were open so, the sounds could be heard upon the small dirt path that separated the shanty neighborhood from the bus terminal. It was the sound of *telenovela* damsels, heroes, and villains. Marco swiftly moved past the non-existing screen door through the wide-open entryway. As his boots announced his presence, the woman on the couch holding a cigarette in one hand and a TV remote in the other jumped higher than she could have ever intended to elevate her obviously obese figure seemingly suffocating her small frame. She let out such a yelp that it seemed she had jumped straight into an ice-cold bath, eyes closed. Marco quickly subdued her and pinned her down on the sofa, looking around for signs of others in the house. No one else seemed to be there.

"Is there anyone else here?"

"No. Please don't hurt me. I have no money!"

"Shut up! Just answer my questions. Nothing more, nothing less from your mouth. Okay? Is that old man over at the station your father?"

"Yes."

"And do you have children, a disabled mother here at home, or a similarly crippled husband that you take care of?"

"No."

"Then what the hell are you doing sitting around on your fat ass wasting your life watching this mind-numbing filth on the television when you haven't taken the time to tend to your father's needs? Are you aware that he has soiled himself? He's been sitting in his own shit so long it's probably hardened like cement by now."

"I didn't know. I check him whenever I can. He is very careless. He's always shitting himself. I'm the only one who takes care of him," responded the woman, her voice cracking.

"That's how you take care of the man who gave you your life? The man who raised you and probably worked hard to give you everything you needed to grow up and choose to be the pathetic person that you are? Is that it? Is that what you want to tell me? That you take care of him by putting him on a chair out there to beg for money so you can sit around doing not a goddamned thing but growing fatter by the minute? And then you don't even care to make sure the poor old man is clean and comfortable?"

"I am trying to do the best I can but sometimes it is just too much. Sometimes I secretly wish he would just die. It's not fair that I have to live my life only to change crapped underwear and care for a cripple!"

Having heard her response Marco instantly lit up with rage, like a blowtorch ready to melt down a non-cooperative bolt rusted and stuck in its ways. He pulled the revolver from his belt. Its silvery skin briefly shining as he held it up over his shoulder allowing the light of the TV to grace its smooth surface. Then he pressed it against the woman's temple.

"Listen to me, you sorry excuse for offspring. I am only going to warn you once. You will get your sorry ass off this couch and make sure that old man over there is very well taken care of from now on. He will have no need to crap himself, and if he does, you will clean him immediately. And speaking of crap, you will never tune his TV to any fucking *telenovela* anymore. Do you understand me? I will be coming by here to check up on him. You won't know when. It could be tomorrow, or it could be next year. But if when I do decide to swing by again, I find out that he's been neglected, I will take this gun and shove it so far up your ass you'll taste the metal. Do I make myself clear?"

"Yes," the woman replied trembling in horror.

"Yes what?"

"Uhh, yyyes...yes, sir."

"Attagirl."

70

He slapped the woman lightly on the cheek with the tip of the gun then got up and put his gun away. He was about to walk out but he noticed that her eyes nervously switched back and forth from his gaze over to the telenovela which had been playing on the TV in the background. He turned around to face the television set and, as if in a western movie, he stood with his feet astride, his hand twitching a little, his jaw tensing up, then suddenly he sprang into action drawing his gun and unloading on the television set a full five rounds until his barrel smoked at the end. There was a slight grin on his face as he slowly turned his head over to the horrified woman still paralyzed on the couch and said with an almost coquettish gesture "You're welcome."

Marco put away his gun and had taken a few steps toward the door, then stopped. He looked frozen as if a sudden thought had hit him. He slowly turned his head to look at the woman on the couch. This gave her chills that surged up and down her spine. It was a strange sensation for her of both fear and attraction.

"I hope you know none of this is personal," he said now speaking in a more compassionate tone. "People need to wake up. We have all been sleeping for so long. No one sees what is really going on. If they only knew, hardly anyone could sit idly by. The sky is falling, raining ashes across the land and no one seems to care. Have you noticed the ash rain? People are suffering and all others think of is the latest episode of their favorite *telenovela*. The world is coming to an end, and people are still sleeping. Just sleeping...It's time to wake the world up...Do you understand?"

The woman silently assented with a few hard nods. Her wide eyes making it obvious that she was still terrified beyond her wit's end.

"My apologies. I have frightened you very much. It was not my intention," Marco spoke making his way to a love seat plopping down on it. He looked at her differently now. His eyes had turned to magnifying glasses that sought to briefly study her. This only served to intensify her feeling of being a little mouse caught between the cat's claws. "You know, your father is confined to that chair out there because of his disability. What confines you to this couch? Don't you have a life? A lover?"

Something in his line of questioning began to bother her, rattling the grit in her heart. She finally found her voice again and spoke up.

"I'm married. We have a son. My husband and our boy went to *el norte* over two years ago to *los Estados Unidos*. I would have gone with them, but..."

"But your father..."

"Yes. He has no one else. All my brothers and sisters have gone their separate ways. No one comes to visit us."

"Does your husband send you money from *el otro lado*?"

"He used to..." her voice unexpectedly broke into a whimper transitioning into sobs. "I haven't heard from them in more than six months. I'm afraid something bad has happened to them. They would not just stop calling. Something must be terribly wrong, and I don't know what to do."

To his surprise, Marco felt a tear fall from his eye which brought him back from an imagined scenario he had pictured as he listened to her story. There was no telling what could have happened to her family, but given the information he had uncovered in his investigations, it was possible that her husband and son had been caught up in one of those undocumented immigrant roundups that were running rampant throughout the U.S. but which no one in the media treated as newsworthy. This in spite of the fact that many times those roundups pulled not only undocumented people, but also residents and even citizens whose only crime was being brown and looking Mexican. What happened to those people after being apprehended, no one really knew. No one seemed to care.

Marco got up and sat next to her. He put his arm around her to console her and as he did this, she broke down even further into a full wailing.

"Jesus. You know, I don't know what the hell I'm doing out here anymore. I've been under so much stress. I, too, have lost my loved ones. My family. The woman I love. Only difference between you and me is that I am the one who has gone missing in their lives...for good."

He touched her chin and lifted her face until their eyes met.

"I hope you get to see your husband and son again soon. Things are going to change for people like them. You'll see. For the better. Here..." he took some cash from his pocket and placed it in her hand. "For your troubles," he said, rising to his feet. "I must go now. I wish you good luck. Don't forget, your father awaits. Take care of him. Life is not guaranteed...not these days."

He stepped out of the house and the woman could see him from her window as he sprinted back toward the bus station. He waved at the driver who had been waiting for him by the door. They both jumped into the bus that had been idling with the interior lamps lit up as passengers rested their heads on backrests and against windows trying to sleep as they waited to depart.

On the road again, Marco found his seat all to himself as he had left it. He was settling back into a comfortable position looking out through the window. The thoughts of the old man at the bus station and his daughter were still on his mind. The faceless images of the woman's husband and son, too, begged to be spared a minute to contemplate. But Marco was feeling a bit selfish, however, because in the back of his mind the thoughts of Sally still held sway. He settled into his seat with the express purpose of reaching back into his past and revisiting his love as he had been doing on that trip. Marco was just beginning to reach his destination in his mind when he felt another person abruptly sitting beside him on the empty aisle seat. He looked over to find a man wearing a black cowboy hat and a leather jacket with strips of rattle snake stitched across the shoulders. He had not bothered to turn and look at Marco who was trying his hardest to shoot lasers from his eyes hoping to get the man to cede the seat and look for another one.

"The seat is taken," Marco finally said forcefully.

"Really?" The man replied with eyes still looking straight ahead. The snarky tone in the man's voice more than anything is what made Marco fume. "I guess you're right. It is taken. By me, that is."

"What did you say?"

The man finally turned to look at him straight in the eyes and Marco instantly knew that this was no ordinary passenger.

"There are a lot of other seats. I am kindly asking you to pick another one. Surely that is not too much to ask." Marco was secretly wrapping his hand on the butt of his revolver and lightly caressing the trigger as he said this.

"I don't think I will. This one is just the one I was recommended."

"Recommended by whom?"

"I'm going to cut to the chase, *amigo*. I followed you from Tamaulipas, where you shot up that bus station. My boss didn't take too kindly to that act. So now the question is, who put you up to it?"

****

Chapter 6
"Miércoles de Ceniza (Ash Wednesday)"

The grounds of the *Televisiva* television and recording studios are comprised of several acres of land segregated from the rest of the City of Mexico by a seven-foot-high concrete wall that surrounds the entire triple football field-sized enclosure. The differences between the sights within those walls and outside are stark. Inside there is lush foliage, vibrant green plants and radiantly colorful flowers. There is landscaping so well perpetrated that the grass looks like carpet and the hedges and bushes look like plush, fluffy stuffed animals. Indeed, those plants and trees are shaped in such a way as to depict ducks and eagles, turtles and a whole host of different wildlife. It seems even the air is cooler within those walls. Whereas—by contrast—outside of that enclosure things get a bit harsher, hotter, and generally much more unpleasant. It is truly a concrete jungle, hardly any green plants are seen around. Multitudes of vehicles and people moving about, selling, stealing, begging, pushing, shoving, grinning, spitting fire, and forcibly washing windshields for a *peso* or a curse. It is chaos compared to the tranquility and order of the *Televisiva* compound.

On TV sets across the nation a message was being broadcast live the morning after Marco's arrival from the Televisiva studios announcing the beginning of the news hour with one of Mexico's preeminent news anchors, Raul Jacobi; a mild-looking man in his late forties but still retaining dark black hair. He was slim and of average height with light skin and brown eyes. Raul always wore a black suit and black tie against a white shirt. He was a clean-cut, dry man; a product of the conservative, strict culture that characterized the politics of the nation as it did the news organizations that covered it.

DESDE LA CAPITAL DE MEXICO,

* *NOTICIERO TELEVISIVA**

CON

RAUL JACOBI

With the precision and timing of a well calibrated machine, Raul began his discourse the instant the camera man dropped his hand pointing a finger at him to indicate that they had gone live.

"Good morning, and welcome to this, your *Noticiero Televisiva*. I am Raul Jacobi, at your service," he said. This was his standard opening line.

"We begin this morning with the strange case of the 'television executioner.' That is correct; a man who 'kills' television sets. Reports have been coming in about a stranger who enters public places such as restaurants and hair salons brandishing a gun seemingly for the sole purpose of shooting and destroying television sets. Authorities have been unable to identify the man other than by tying him to a string of similar incidents occurred along our border with the U.S. in the states of Tamaulipas and Texas respectively. Officers of the Borderland Police and our own State of Mexico Police Department say they do not have a motive, nor a suspect. They speculate that it could be a rather benign form of intimidation by cartels to instill fear on businesses that do not cooperate with a monthly quota. Other officers posit that perhaps it is a head game on the part of one cartel against other cartels, since the string of incidents can be traced from San Antonio, Texas, a known cartel drug corridor, to our own City of Mexico. Yet other voices, all speaking on condition of anonymity, stated to *Noticiero Televisiva* that it could be a case of a failed TV star out for symbolic payback, since it appears that witnesses have testified in every incident that the stranger shot out the television sets while a *Televisiva telenovela* was in progress.

For more on this case we welcome Juan Jose de la Espada Andrade who is covering the story and will be presenting his full report this evening in the prime-time news hour at 6. Juan Jose, welcome. What will you have for us tonight?"

On their screens, the TV audience could see the images shift from Raul to a pudgy-looking reporter standing at the edge of the lake in Chapultepec park overseeing Mexico's high rises in the background. He was Juan Jose, the correspondent to whom Raul would always go to first in his news hour. Juan Jose was the direct opposite of Raul. Dark skin, round belly, sloppy dresser, always looking like he had just thrown on his clothes from the dirty pile. But, otherwise, a good correspondent, and a familiar face on Mexican screens.

"Good morning, Raul. And a very good morning to our beloved television viewers and compatriots throughout the nation," Juan Jose replied. This was his own standard opening one-liner.

"Indeed, we have much more to cover in this ongoing case. For the moment, I can inform you that I have spoken to officers of the Borderland Police, the State Municipal Police, the *procuraduria general*, and others all of whom concur on only a few details such as that it seems to be a one-man act, seemingly the same man, since it has been noted that he targets television sets and not people. Another distinguishing feature in this case is the gun, which witnesses in several of the locales have stated is a revolver. Some witnesses have also identified the man as possessing a long beard on at least two of the incidents, although this is not corroborated by other sightings which point to him being a clean-shaven individual. We will have full coverage of this strange case later tonight on the *Noticiero Nocturno* at 6 pm. We will discuss the latest incident occurred just last night here in the City of Mexico at a bus terminal involving two men, one of whom seemed to be holding the other at gunpoint as they boarded a shuttle to a local hotel. The incident was captured on video and posted to social media spurring speculation that, perhaps, this could have been the television shooter, since it happened at another bus station, as occurred in Tamaulipas. Some have countered this theory by pointing out in the comments, however, that it couldn't have been the same gunman, since he clearly did not shoot any television sets. For now, that is all. From Chapultepec park in the *Ciudad de Mexico*, for *Noticiero Televisiva*, I am Juan Jose de la Espada Andrade. Back to you in the studio."

Raul shifted on his seat to face the camera to his left, transitioning from that segment.

"Thanks very much to our correspondent and colleague, Juan Jose," he said.

"We look forward to his full report tonight. In other, possibly related news, officials of the Narco Drug Task Force of the Borderland Police report this morning that a gruesome discovery has been made by locals in the state of Tamaulipas at a factory warehouse."

On viewers' screens, video images of the dead replaced the polished look of Raul and the neat news desk from which he described the scene. The warehouse where the massacre had taken place was located just blocks away from the border bus station Marco had shot up days prior, which had prompted the narco turf war escalation.

"Officials say that as many as fifteen men were found murdered, all believed to be members of the two most powerful narco cartels of the north, one run by a boss known as *el Zapo Tote*, and the other run by a boss known as *el Comander*. All of the delinquents were found riddled with bullets and every single one also shot in the head, execution style. Officials stated off the record that they believe that also among the dead were none other than the kingpins *Zapo To*te and *Comander* themselves. Authorities have speculated that perhaps this could have been a cartel coup orchestrated by members of one or both cartels to eliminate the old order. We'll bring you more details as they develop. And now for the weather report we go to Maria Azul Mendiola, who has an update for us on the ongoing ash rain phenomenon taking place throughout the country. Adelante, Maria. "

The news hour progressed in usual fashion until its conclusion. As Raul signed off and the cameras ended their broadcast, a woman of small stature but larger than life personality burst through the double door entrance into the recording studio. Her name was Raquel Usaman, the producer and host of the hit show "*El Sexto Sol*," (The Sixth Sun). It was a show on the topic of strange news and mysterious phenomena covered in an expository fashion giving it a sense of legitimacy and credibility. She was loud, announcing herself as she approached the set to prepare for her program almost pushing the Raul Jacobi Noticiero Televisiva group out of the way.

"More conspiracy theories to report on, I suspect?" said Raul disparagingly as he handed over his cordless mic to one of the staff. He was purposely slow to rise out of his chair and vacate the desk on set.

Raquel mockingly froze in her tracks feigning complete surprise as she looked at Raul.

"*Dios mío*, the robot has the capacity of independent speech? I thought you were limited to your script! Good for you, my boy. Good for you," she said, taking the seat and swiping away onto the floor some papers Raul had left behind on the desk.

"It's time to take apart the echo chamber, gentlemen!" Raquel shouted at her team as she watched Raul exit the studio with a sour look on his face. She winked and smirked at him sending him off fuming at her irreverence.

If you are one of the millions of viewers of "El Sexto Sol" from across the Americas and the world, when you tune in on streaming services, cable, or broadcast television, the sequence that constitutes the show's introduction is a montage of images of old world travelers to the new world, the fall of Tenochtitlan, the Mexican Revolution, the industrial revolution, and the information age, all capped at the end by the camera taking flight over the Gulf of Mexico toward the east and ending with a fiercely bright rising sun with the show's title across the screen alluding to the promise and ambiguity of what the future will bring.

Raquel always begins at the top of the show the way she enters a room: she pivots aggressively toward the camera with a loud, attention-grabbing shout saying, "*Hoy*!" or "Today!"

"*Hoy*! On El Sexto Sol. We will explore strange phenomena and mysterious happenings. But we will break with our usual format to present to you a special segment. A segment I call, 'Once Upon A Time in Tenochtitlan.' Today as always, we will dispel myths, dispense with propaganda, and disrupt paradigms to bring you the unfiltered, raw truth of history, the current world we live in, and the future that awaits us. And ladies and gentlemen, the future…is here."

Raquel rose from her chair at the news desk and walked to an open area of the stage where a screen lit up to reveal images of Mexico City's Zocalo, the city's main square. In the background was the Metropolitan Cathedral. It was clear that it was stock video footage because the image began to melt as it transformed into a reconstruction of the sacred precinct or central plaza of the ancient city of Tenochtitlan.

"Once upon a time in Tenochtitlan…" she addressed the camera now in a more measured tone.

Across town in the city center at the Mexiqui Zocalo hostel, Marco sat in the middle of a room fitted with three metal-framed bunk beds usually rented out to groups of six men for a low flat rate per night. It's a great deal if you can find vacancy, because it's right in the center of the city in the heart of ancient Tenochtitlan (for those inclined to take the one-minute walk over to the Templo Mayor ruins).

"You guarantee that you didn't tell Raquel our exact location?" Marco inquired, addressing the camera crew that had just finished setting up their lights and cameras, and getting him ready to go live on El Sexto Sol.

"Yes. All she knows is that we are with you. We're getting a hold of her as we speak. You'll be going live in moments…" said the producer who had introduced himself as Miguel. He suddenly paused and looked up at the top bed of a bunk which was positioned against a green wall. On the wall was painted a mural of a modern woman blowing a gum bubble and wearing a Jaguar Knight head dress, fangs perched up against her forehead.

The cameraman looked back at Marco and asked, "You sure your buddy there isn't going to get up any time soon? If he were to just jump off the bed in the middle of the shoot, he could ruin our segment."

Marco looked up at the man in the top bunk who seemed to be sound asleep, and with a smirk he looked back at the cameraman saying, "Believe me, he won't. He's dead asleep."

"Must have been a heavy night of partying you both had last night, huh?" said the cameraman.

"Yeah," Marco replied pensively, "something like that."

The man on the bunk was none other than the cowboy who had taken over the isle seat on the bus the day before, when Marco was still en-route to the Mexican capital. They had ridden a shuttle straight from the station to the Mexiqui Zocalo hostel, where the cowboy would hold Marco while he waited for some of his associates to arrive in the city. What the cowboy had not anticipated was that Marco had already made other plans. He had contacted El Sexto Sol days earlier from the road with the promise of highly valuable footage detailing evidence in support of a conspiracy theory that Raquel herself had spouted on the show in previous occasions regarding the phenomenon of disappearing immigrants in the U.S., and the mysterious ashfall throughout both countries. Marco was not willing to let this man disrupt his plan to expose the truth to the world. Although he had relinquished his gun to the cowboy before they exited the bus at the terminal after discovering that his unwelcome seat companion had been pointing his own pistol at him, Marco didn't turn over the dagger he carried strapped to his calf. Once inside their room at the hostel, in a brief distraction,

Marco quickly sprung out his dagger and slit the cowboy's throat. He wrapped him in a sheet and hurled him up to the top bunk where he slowly bled to death over night as Marco leaned sleeplessly against a window overlooking the Zocalo, while chain-smoking the short, flavorful Raleigh cigarettes he'd picked up at the Mexiqui Zocalo café downstairs.

Back at Televisiva Studios, Raquel was part through her opening monologue:

"It happened in the times of Moctezuma, ladies and gentlemen. Strange phenomena seen across the land. Inexplicable sightings of objects in the sky, mysterious plagues, creatures of lore coming to life to terrorize nocturnal life in the great metropolis…and then, the end of the world!" Raquel dragged out the last four words for maximum dramatization as images of Aztec codices flashed on the screen behind her depicting the events she was describing in stark fashion.

"So, the question is, are we not looking at a similar fate? The ancients believed that life is cyclical. That what has happened before will happen again. Are we not staring into the abyss? Are we not living in dark times of turmoil and tribulation? The signs are all around us. Un-identified flying objects, strange creatures terrorizing cattle, mysterious diseases springing out of nowhere, and now this ash that keeps falling and no one knows where it is coming from. Last week, penitents crawling on their knees across the Zocalo toward the

Metropolitan Cathedral were greeted by clergymen granting them the ash cross markings on the forehead using the ashfall, which was plentiful. It covered the entire plaza! This despite the fact that Ash Wednesday is today. They started putting the cross on people's foreheads early this year, perhaps because of the gravity of the moment. Even the Pope will be making an appearance at the Metropolitan Cathedral later today. This would be his second visit since he was elevated to the Throne of St. Peter. The first time he visited was in 2016..."

The camera zoomed in on her face as Raquel continued:

"Friends, indeed, the times have come full circle. The end time is near. But worry not, for the ancients predicted that this would happen. It was said that a new sun would be born, bringing a new era to humanity. The era of man known as '*El Sexto Sol*'. Yes, this is the source for the title of our show. But this prophecy would not happen until a messenger arrived to deliver a message to the people. For ages, people have waited, speculated, and searched for said messenger to no avail. But, ladies and gentlemen, we must search no more. Here at El Sexto Sol the prophecy has delivered to us the said messenger (as it would seem)..." she said, briefly turning to a side camera to allow a small break in the dramatic tone she had built up, and to encourage the viewers to interpret a slight skepticism on her part. It was a way to allow herself an out in case the story fell flat on account of her guest turning out to be a fraud, which given the nature of the topic for that day, was highly likely.

"And like the clarion in Aztec times who shouted from atop the tallest watch tower in the city: 'Mexicas, your enemies escape!' on the so-called 'Night of Sorrow'…" she continued with the build up to her reveal, "…our guest today comes to us to deliver a message like a clarion call. He has journeyed all the way from the farthest reaches of the United States with evidence that will astound you!"

Raquel turned to the screen behind her, which had been playing images on a loop and now broadcast a live image of Marco sitting in that hostel room.

"Good morning, my friend. It's an honor to have you with us today," she said, welcoming Marco to the show. He, for his part, simply nodded but said nothing.

Turning to the camera, Raquel quipped raising an eyebrow, "A man of few words, I see." She gave a comedic stare into the camera, as a cartoon character with a zipper across its mouth seemed to float across the screen spoofing Marco's tight-lipped greeting. Only viewers at home would have seen that animation on their screens. Marco had no idea that this was part of the show's format. It was, yet again, another way for Raquel and her team to disown any stories that ended up being discredited, as well as adding an element of entertainment best suited for short clips posted to the show's social media accounts.

"You contacted us days ago, and—I should mention—you didn't share your name with me. This is why I did not introduce you to our audience by name. I'm sure you'll get to that on your own time. However, you explained that you are—excuse me, were—a journalist in your past life in the United States. And it is this very profession that led you to make some very profoundly disturbing discoveries, didn't it?"

"Yes," Marco said, appearing momentarily camera shy.

"Very well, we will explore that in a bit. But before we do, I'd like to ask you a straightforward question. *Sin rodeos.* Are you familiar with the news stories of the 'Television Hitman'?"

Marco seemed to be caught off guard by this. He had not mentioned anything to her about this aspect of himself.

"Television hitman?" he responded incredulously.

"Yes. I have a feeling it was you. Call it a hunch. I am, after all, a reporter myself, you know…"

She paused to address the audience with a look directly at the camera in the studio, and then she turned back to the screen and continued,

"It was you, wasn't it? It was odd to me that you contacted us from the road as you did. We checked the phone number you used to call us. It was a public phone in a Tamaulipas bus station. I thought that was interesting, given the reports of the Television Hitman shooting up that same bus station on that same day. Frankly, if it hadn't been for you sending me the short clip of the video you have in your possession, I would have just ignored you like all the rest of the loonies that try to get on my show."

A cartoon of a raving mad lunatic in a strait jacket bounced around viewers' screens as Raquel continued,

"But then I thought, even if he hadn't shared the clip, I still would have him on my show so we can finally unmask the notorious TV Hitman! But the question is, why risk all the attention? If you have such an important, urgent message for us, why would you risk jeopardizing it all?"

"Well, I…I am that man…" said Marco defeatedly.

"Ah-ha! Breaking news, ladies and gentlemen! You saw it here first. We have solved the mystery of the Television Hitman!"

"Yes. It is true. I did it to call attention to the very same message I have here to present on your show. But I will not disclose the video footage until I have a couple of minutes of your time to speak directly to your audience, as we agreed to on the phone the day we spoke."

"Of course, my friend. I am a woman of my word. The floor is yours," Raquel said this as a cartoon of an uninhibited janitor danced across the screen seemingly mopping an invisible floor to the tune of *La Negra Tomasa*.

As Marco was about to speak, the footage of the interview briefly switched from the camera aimed at him, to a live shot of the Zocalo, where a large congregation of people had already begun to amass awaiting the arrival of the Pope. Faintly, too, was the presence in the air of tiny dust which created a hazy atmosphere in the plaza. The camera panned back toward the interior of the room to reveal a look of Marco's back as he sat addressing the show's audience.

"Fellow Mexicans, Americans, and citizens of the world. My name is Marco Angelino. I am a journalist from the United States. My family roots are in Mexico. This is the reason why I have devoted much of my professional work to topics relating to U.S. and Mexico relations. In the course of this work I have made a troubling discovery. Something which should be of grave concern for all people of Mexican origins, and for all humanity. On me I have definitive proof certain members of our current government in the United States acting in secret have not only verbally declared their goal of finding a solution to what they call the Mexican problem, but also evidence of that aim being met by the creation of a new super weapon. A weapon more powerful and more dangerous than any bomb or weapon of war man has ever invented. This tool of devastation can function remotely and undetectably. It gives its possessor the power to eliminate anyone anywhere in a split second leaving no trace but a pile of ashes. The exact nature of this weapon is unknown. How it is deployed, where it is housed, or when it will be used for maximum effect, as they have said they intend to, are also unknown. But one thing is for sure: it exists. And it is likely the cause of the ashfall across both our nations."

Marco paused briefly and looked down as if to collect his thoughts. He then looked back up into the camera as he continued,

"Ladies and gentlemen, there is no mystery about the ashfall, not anymore. I traveled here personally to deliver the proof to the Mexican people and to the world, because I knew that putting forth my face and my identity would be the only way to lend credibility to this very real threat. We can no longer afford to keep watching their *telenovelas*, their propaganda, their programming designed to keep us blind to the truth. Wasting away in front of our televisions, while all around us the ash keeps falling, and more and more of our displaced compatriots go missing and no one knows where they are. No one seems to care…"

At the Televisiva studio, Raquel stood next to the screen showing images of Marco speaking mixed with stock images of human sacrifice from post-conquest codices, and live footage of the Zocalo outside of the Mexiqui hostel. Marco pressed on with his monologue:

"...My father had a saying when I was growing up: 'The world ends for those who die.' Well, Mexicans, we are all about to die! It's the end of the world. It's time to get mad and change the channel, change your life! The last thing you need is to watch another telenovela. Wake up and live. There isn't much time left for us. But I will say no more. I will show you the proof now. Permit me a moment..."

Marco stood up from the chair, removing the microphone which had been attached to his lapel. The mobile camera took over filming Marco as he stepped away toward a door. In the studio, Raquel seemed perplexed as this unscripted moment in the interview unraveled. But her news reporter senses quickly kicked into gear and she began to address the producer on site.

"Miguel, can you tell us anything about what just happened? What's behind that door?"

"Well, Raquel. It appears that our guest has just gone into the restroom. It is also a communal shower room here at the Mexiqui Zocalo hostel. It is shared by all the guests on this floor."

"While we wait for Mr. Angelino to come back, why don't you tell us a bit more about him. What was your first impression when you arrived at that location?"

"Of course," said Miguel. "When we arrived, he met us outside and led us up to this room. As you witnessed for yourself, he seemed very mysterious. He's very quiet. Speaks only when necessary. We began setting up and then I noticed his friend sleeping up on the top bunk up there..." the camera swung around to reveal the lump on the top bunk that was supposed to be Marco's "friend" sleeping off a hangover. He continued,

"I asked if he could wake his friend and tell him to wait outside to avoid interrupting his interview if he were to wake up suddenly during the shoot. But, you know, the strangest thing about it is that he hasn't snored or moved at all since we got here."

"I suppose he must have gotten a little carried away last night with the Tequila. After all, it is Mexico City," Raquel commented, shifting the focus without a segue back to the topic of Marco's journey through the U.S. and into Mexico.

"It's curious, and I think you and our audience will agree, Miguel, how Mr. Angelino was able to cause all that mayhem shooting TV sets throughout various parts of both sides of the border and yet not a single law enforcement official was able to capture him, or give as much as a brief comment as to the mystery behind this man. Don't you think, Miguel?"

"Yes. You're absolutely right, Raquel. It is interesting. To me it looks like someone who, for some reason, wanted to get caught, and like you said, nobody seemed to care enough to track him and capture him. Maybe it was the fact that in all the incidents there were no reported deaths. But, still, it's odd."

"Indeed…" Raquel added. She paused pensively, then turned back to the screen where Miguel stood looking expectantly into the camera.

"Miguel, if you will, take us closer to the door. He mentioned that he would show us the evidence now. I suppose he had it hidden in there. Let's ask him about it."

The cameraman approached the door to the restroom revealing his shadow as he closed in and leaned against it. A sudden burst became audible to the camera crew, which Miguel mentioned whispering into the camera.

"Raquel, it seems something has happened. I don't know what. It was a sound like something blowing up but making only a muffled sound."

Intrigued, Raquel responded,

"Miguel, can you knock on the door? Let's see if our guest will answer."

Miguel knocked twice on the door but heard no response. After a short while, Raquel again asked him to act.

"Miguel, see if you can open the door. Is it locked? If not, try entering the room."

Miguel took the handle, while his assistant cameraman recorded every tense moment from behind. As they opened the unlocked door, Miguel snuck his head in partially, allowing the cameraman space to do the same with the camera. He called out:

"Mr. Angelino? Is everything okay?"

Not a word came back. But at that moment, as if a light breeze had blown from within the restroom, a cloud of grey ash engulfed the camera and Miguel, who momentarily jumped back. In the studio, Raquel was completely transfixed, both because the scene was riveting, but also because she knew that this was a ratings-spiking moment sent from heaven to boost her show like no other story had done.

"Mr. Angelino?" Miguel asked again. This time he stuck his arm out into the view of the camera and pushed the door wide open. With Miguel in the lead, they entered the room which was now fully covered in floating ash. Miguel continued to call out for Marco to no avail. Then, as he crept slowly further into the large communal restroom, he saw a pile of ashes on the ground that seemed to be the epicenter of the muted pop they had heard. He kneeled next to it and instinctively reached into the pile with his fingers for the television viewers to see as he probed the ashes. To his surprise, Miguel retrieved a micro SD card from the ash pile. The camera turned to him as his face looked up in awe and he lifted the SD card into view.

"Raquel," said Miguel again almost in a whisper.

"*Dime* Miguel. What are we looking at?"

"It is a memory card. A storage device."

"Could this be where our guest carried his proof, Miguel?" she asked in a tone cleverly intended to add to the suspense of her viewers.

"I'd say so," he responded absentmindedly.

"Can you see where he could have gone? Perhaps he climbed out a window and blew up some homemade firecracker just for the theatrical effect?"

"I suppose it is a possibility," said Miguel, as he looked up at a small window situated about seven feet high on the wall. It was possible that Marco had escaped through that window, although it was closed, with the latch in lock position. It would have been impossible for Marco to have locked the window if he was on the outside, Miguel thought.

"Miguel, can you explore the contents of the memory card at this moment for our viewers?" Raquel said, breaking his chain of thoughts.

"Certainly," Miguel responded.

They stepped back into the room where they had set up for the interview. As Miguel set upon inserting the memory card into the laptop he carried, Raquel came on again with another request.

"*Amigos*, let us see again the view from the balcony overlooking the plaza."

Taking the directorial cue from Raquel, the mobile camera began making its way out onto the balcony again, but before the cameraman exited the room, he noticed the lump on the top bunk had begun to seep blood through the sheets. He stopped and focused on the bed as Miguel came up from behind:

"Oh my God!" Miguel said as he realized what had occurred. He stepped into the shot and removed the sheet to reveal the corpse of the cowboy with his throat slit wide open. Before they could discuss their morbid finding a commotion seemed to be stirring outside in the main plaza.

The cameraman did not wait for direction this time, as he instinctively rushed outside onto the balcony overlooking the Zocalo. By this time, the visibility over the plaza had been significantly reduced given the noticeable increase in ashfall. Nonetheless, it was possible to see that the crowds had grown enormously. As the camera panned across the plaza toward the Metropolitan Cathedral, a shocking scene began to unfold on live television. Several of the penitents on the plaza began to shake and abruptly blow up into what looked like big puffs of smoke right where they stood. At first it was one man. Then, a couple of random people at the same time. Suddenly, they began popping like kernels of corn in hot oil. An audible shrill could be heard across the Zocalo as the panic-gripped multitudes began to run in every direction, all the while still popping into clouds of ash one by one, unable to outrun their impending demise. The cameraman quickly shifted around toward the interior of the room where Miguel still stood transfixed by the corpse and called out to him.

"Miguel!"

As Miguel looked up, he could see clearly the shock in his assistant's face. Before he could ask what was happening, a loud pop was heard and the camera dropped straight down to the floor still filming and pointing toward Miguel, but now only half of his body could be seen in the footage. He was making his way to the balcony when, in front of the live streaming camera, before the millions of television viewers and Raquel in the studio, who by now was speechless, Miguel appeared like a Black Cat firecracker popping into a cloud of ash spreading in all directions.

With the live feed abruptly cut, the programming returned to Raquel in the studio. Her eyes nearly bursting out of her sockets, unblinking. Her jaw dropped, seemingly just hanging by a thread. She was, for the first time ever on her show, at a total loss for words. But her inner showman's voice reminded her of the number one rule of live television: the show must go on. And with a trembling jaw, her voice cracking as she struggled to keep it together, she managed to close the segment with a sense of normalcy that did not match her demeanor, nor the footage viewers had just witnessed:

"*Damas y Caballeros*. This has been a production of '*El Sexto Sol*.' I am your host Raquel Usaman. And now…a word from our sponsors."

Just as the footage of the show was about to switch from the image of Raquel standing next to the now blank screen behind her to the sponsor's messages, a loud pop was heard, leaving television viewers glued to their screens, suffering through every second of those commercials just to confirm, when the programming returned, if Raquel herself had blown up on the studio floor. A full two thirds of the show's viewers across the globe that day were never able to find out the answer to this or any other question in life…

Gabriel Hugo is the author of Once Upon a Bad Hombre, the X Series, The Martian Ones, and The Fluid Chicano. He has collaborated with authors on several anthologies and his poetry has been featured in various literary publications. Gabriel is also the founder of The Raving Press, an independent publishing imprint in the Rio Grande Valley, publishing works primarily focused on issues affecting Chicanos and other minorities in the United States. He is also an actor, appearing in two films available on Amazon Prime Video. Gabriel Hugo lives in Mission, Texas with his two sons Hugo Kuahutemoc and Jose Moctezuma, a.k.a. "The Bro Team". For more visit: http://gabrielhugo.com/